E YOU ON OUR EMAIL LIST?
SIGN UP ON OUR WEBSITE
v.thecartelpublications.com
OR TEXT THE WORD:
CARTELBOOKS TO **22828**
R PRIZES, CONTESTS, ETC.

By T. Styles

PRETTY KINGS III

Denim's Blues

T. STYLES

NATIONAL BEST SELLING AUTHOR OF *RAUNCHY*

CHECK OUT OTHER TITLES BY THE CARTEL PUBLICATIONS

PRISON THRONE
GOON
HOETIC JUSTICE
THE END. HOW TO WRITE A BESTSELLING NOVEL IN 30 DAYS
WWW.THECARTELPUBLICATIONS.COM

By T. Styles

Pretty Kings 3: Denim's Blues

By T. Styles

PUBLISHER'S NOTE:
This book is a work of fiction. Names, characters,
businesses,
Organizations, places, events and incidents are the
product of the
Author's imagination or are used fictionally. Any re-
semblance of
Actual persons, living or dead, events, or locales are
entirely coincidental.

Library of Congress Control Number: 2014954695

ISBN 10: 0989790193

ISBN 13: 978-0989790192

Cover Design: Davida Baldwin www.oddballdsgn.com
Editor(s): T. Styles, C. Wash, S. Ward
www.thecartelpublications.com
First Edition
Printed in the United States of America

What's Up Fam,

I hope everybody's transition from Summer to Fall 2014 has been a smooth one. This is the time of year I love! The weather is not too cold and not too hot, the holidays are right around the corner and its FOOTBALL season! #CowboysRavensNation. Don't worry, you read it correctly I am a HUGE Dallas Cowboys and Baltimore Ravens fan. Two teams may not be for everybody, but it works for me ;)

On to the novel in hand, "Pretty Kings: 3 Denim's Blues". Mannnnnnn, this installment is easily my favorite one of the Pretty Kings series. T. Styles has done an excellent job of weaving a beautiful drama filled story together that catches us up, keeps us guessing what's gonna happen next and she sprinkles in the perfect amount of surprises that I promise you will NOT see coming. Buckle up cause you in for a ride!

Keeping in line with tradition, we want to give respect to a vet or trailblazer paving the way. With that said we would like to recognize:

Steve Harvey

Steve Harvey's not only an original Kings of Comedy comedian, game show, radio and talk show host, he is also a New York Times bestselling author. His latest novel, "Act Like A Success, Think Like A Success" has quickly become one of my favorite books. Steve really stresses the point of finding your gift and your purpose no matter what it may be and being successful in it. Trust me, no matter if you are a CEO of a Fortune 500 company or a maid in a hotel, pick this book up and start your journey toward greatness.

Aight, get to it. I'll get at you in the next novel.

Be Easy!

Charisse "C. Wash" Washington
Vice President
The Cartel Publications
www.thecartelpublications.com
www.facebook.com/publishercwash
Instagram: publishercwash
www.twitter.com/cartelbooks
www.facebook.com/cartelpublications
Follow us on Instagram: Cartelpublications

Dedications

I dedicate this novel to all my fans near and far.

#prettykings3

By T. Styles

PROLOGUE

*B*ambi Kennedy saw prisms of red, green and white as Bradley Kennedy tightened the grasp he held on her neck. Salty sweat poured off his forehead and dripped into her widened eyes as he squeezed harder.

He had one intention in mind.

To kill her.

The mattress under their bodies squeaked quietly as he proceeded with his mission. With each squeeze, Bambi could feel the breath being extracted from her lungs and her body collapsing. Glancing up into her brother-in-law's eyes, panic gripped her because although she knew him for years, at the moment, she didn't recognize him.

He was supposed to love her.

He was family.

Suddenly Bambi felt warm liquid dampen her thigh and when she fixed her gaze in that direction, she saw that it was Bradley. He wanted to kill her so badly that he lost control of his bladder and urinated over her legs.

Her chest felt weighted as she saw the vein down the middle of his forehead pulsate while his face reddened.

Bambi thought about her family. She thought about her life and she thought about all of the things she had to do before exiting this world. She wasn't prepared to leave things undone.

Not now.

Not like this.

In an attempt to save her own life, Bambi scratched at his arms and face, taking skin and blood with each thrash. When he showed no signs of slacking up, she slammed closed fists against his jaw. No matter how hard she fought, nothing seemed to work. At the end of the day, although she was strong, she was reminded that he was a man and she was a woman.

With one more idea in mind, she raised her right knee and banged it into his penis with all of her might.

In extreme pain, he released his hold momentarily and Bambi rolled off the bed and her body collided with the floor. On her hands and knees, she coughed a few times and used the wall to stand up as she struggled to pull air back into her lungs. No sooner than she was on her feet, Bradley was behind her again.

With her slender neck in the pit of his forearm, he flexed his bicep and squeezed in an effort to complete the task he started...the murder of Bambi Kennedy.

By T. Styles

CHAPTER ONE
DENIM
SIX MONTHS EARLIER

The sky was clear and a cool breeze rushed through my moist dreads.

I was so fucking anxious.

As I stood in front of the prison, I kept rubbing my sweaty hands on my thighs. Trying to speed things up in my mind, I closed and opened my eyes so many times hoping he'd appear, that my head throbbed. I couldn't believe this day finally arrived.

Where was he?

The anticipation was killing me.

After so much time, my husband was coming home to me!

So much happened in my life over the past year that I didn't think God fucked with me anymore. First, my baby girl Jasmine was killed in a fire at our house. There was no greater pain than dealing with the loss of a child and I was still not myself.

A little while after that, Bradley was arrested for allegedly raping my sister. Although I knew Bradley wasn't capable of sexual abuse against Grainger because he didn't even like her, he was still in jail for the crime.

Just when I thought God removed him from my life forever, suddenly Grainger went missing and I received notice that he was being released. The reason was simple. If there were no witnesses, they couldn't hold him.

This moment was bittersweet but still I needed to know. Where was my sister?

She had been missing for almost a year and no one heard or saw anything from her. The last time I saw her she was trying to extort money from me to keep Bradley out of jail. I still remember what she said to cause Bradley to steal her in the face with a closed fist.

"You always coming at me about that retarded ass baby of yours," Grainger said to me after we had a disagreement about how she was watching Jasmine. "Can't nobody fuck up that kid more than it's fucked up already," she continued, trying to take jabs at Jasmine for being autistic.

By the time I went to grab her for disrespecting my baby, I saw a blur roll past the side of my face. It was Bradley's fist and it landed directly onto my sister's mouth. Grainger dropped to the floor and I could tell she didn't have use of her lower jaw because her tongue rolled loosely around the walls of her mouth, like a fish.

He broke her jaw.

Even though no one heard from her, it wasn't unlike Grainger to be missing in action. She claimed to be clean off drugs but I'm sure she lied. I figured she ran off with some addict and they were binging.

Yep. Things were definitely heavy in my world, which was why I so desperately needed my husband home.

I turned momentarily and smiled at my family. They were standing in front of a large black Hummer truck, just as excited as I was to see Bradley.

It was Bambi, Scarlett, Race, Camp, Kevin, and Ramirez and they all waved at me. When I glanced up the block I saw six more Hummers parked on the curb. Security was heightened because the beef with the Russians had reached an all-time high.

By T. Styles

I focused back in front of me and a few moments later the large grey gate that held him for almost a year opened. He was coming! Although I couldn't see Bradley yet, my heart didn't know. It beat so heavily that my shirt moved up and down.

And then there he was. Tall and powerful. He appeared poised as he came striding in my direction. Dressed in designer blue jeans, a white t-shirt and a black Tom Ford jacket, he looked like he never did a day behind bars.

My body trembled as he swaggered closer to me, the seat of my panties getting wetter by the step. Months of playing with my pussy had gotten old and it was time for him to take care of business.

Unable to stay away a minute longer, I rushed over to him. A full smile covered my face as I leapt into his arms. He caught me and planted soft kisses all around the tattoos on my neck and along my shoulders.

And as if he just realized that we were back together he put me down and stared deeply into my eyes. It was long and hard. The kind of look that made me say yes when he asked me to be his wife. Slowly he leaned down until our lips were pressed closely together, no air between them.

It was the most passionate kiss I experienced in my life.

Eventually, although I didn't want to, we separated. He snaked his hand around the back of my neck and in a deep whisper said, "You ain't been fucking nobody else have you, bitch?" He squeezed tightly, forcing an electric jolt to course down my back.

I laughed thinking he was joking. It wasn't until I looked at him again that I realized he wasn't.

He leaned in and whispered, so that only I could hear him. "Because I will kill you, Denim. With my bare hands, I swear to God."

I stepped away from him, afraid of how he was coming at me and afraid that I didn't recognize him anymore.

"Can we get some love too?" Kevin said walking up behind me.

I was grateful for the interruption because I was confused. In our entire relationship, I never stepped out on Bradley nor did I think about it. He was everything I ever wanted in a man.

So why the disrespect?

Confused, I moved to the side and watched him interact with his brothers. First, he hugged Kevin, Camp and Ramirez. Then he pulled in Bambi, Scarlett and Race. I wondered was he giving them the third degree too. Or did his distrust stop with me?

"So what's up with the extra security?" Bradley asked as he put his arm around my shoulder. I moved closer to him, still imprisoned by his comment. "It looks like ya'll out here waiting on President Obama to come out this bitch."

"Naw, we was waiting on your punk ass," Kevin joked. His expression turned serious. "A lot of shit going on with the Russians. Things not how they used to be, brother. Don't worry." He slapped him on the back. "We'll update you on all that shit later."

"Yeah, right now we gotta get you home so you can take care of my girl," Bambi said as her long brown hair danced in the wind. She winked at me. "Ain't that right, sis?"

I nodded, still feeling out of it by Bradley's recent remark.

"Home?" Bradley said sarcastically. "Man, I'm 'bout to fuck my wife in the back of one of these

By T. Styles

trucks." He gripped his dick. "The only question I got is who's driving?"

Sarge was piloting the truck as I sat on top of Bradley and winded my hips like the second hand on a clock. Sarge's old ass insisted on playing that old ass Temptations CD he always rocked but it didn't bother me this time.

Bradley was the center of my attention.

Every time he pumped into my body, he looked up into my eyes. I didn't know what was wrong with him earlier when he accused me of being untrue but now we were back.

When Bradley gazed at me I felt bad for those chicks that never had a man look upon them with admiration and lust. I knew my husband loved me. It wasn't in what he said but how he touched me and how me cared for me.

"You feel so fucking good, Denim," he said as he bit down on his bottom lip. "The pussy's as tight as I left it."

"You know I don't play that shit, Bradley. I would never have another man dirtying up my body. I'm yours." I kissed his lips, hoping he'd really believe me. "I ain't even been wearing no tight clothes since you been gone," I said while reveling in his touch. "If you couldn't see my curves I didn't want another nigga doing it either."

That must've been it for him because he snatched me and ran his tongue along the base of my neck. When I felt his teeth bite down on my flesh, I knew he was about to cum.

"Ahhhhhh," he moaned as he gripped my hips and pushed into me harder. Suddenly, he shoved me off and said, "Suck this shit. I want to come on that tongue."

Feeling we were already doing too much with Sarge in the truck, I honored his request. The palms of my hands rested on his kneecaps and my mouth covered his penis. Within seconds, I could feel his cream splash down my throat as he reached an orgasm. It tasted like garlic and salt.

I didn't know how I felt but I tried to put my feelings out of my mind. Ever since Jasmine died, I was emotional and I didn't want to visit my bullshit on my husband.

So I smiled it off and said, "You didn't beat your dick in jail, did you?" I swallowed again to push the nut down the base of my throat. "I can tell."

"If I couldn't cum in you I wasn't gonna cum period." I couldn't stop the grin from rising on my face when I heard his words. He always knew what to say to me. His head turned and he looked out the back window and said, "Get dressed. The fam on their way over here."

I was already pulling up my clothes. I guess Sarge knew we were through because the truck stopped and he parked. When I looked out the back window I saw two more Hummer trucks pull up.

They both were filled with members of my family.

"So what we gonna do now?" Kevin asked.

"Yeah, you done already got the pussy," Ramirez added.

"I say we go to a club or something," Bradley said kissing me again. "I'm home and it's time to celebrate!"

I wanted to go out with them but my plan was to go clean up first but I'm sure we would be at each other again even at the club so there was no use. He was going to have his way with me as many times as he wanted and I wasn't about to complain.

When my phone vibrated, I pulled it out and saw it was a text message from my mother.

Denim cum right away. I need help!

I looked over at Bradley who was already staring at my phone, reading her words. Before he said anything, I immediately knew he would be mad. He and my mother butted heads constantly because in his opinion, she used me. But she was my mother and I couldn't deny her if she needed me.

"I'm sorry, Bradley. I'll meet ya'll after I see what she wants, okay?" I said with a smile, hoping he'd be easy with the situation.

Bradley looked at my family and they backed away from the truck to give us some privacy. "I'm home now, Denim. Do you know what that means?"

"Of course, baby. It means—"

"That I'm going to need all of your attention and I can't have your mother getting in the way of that," he interrupted, squeezing my chin. "I can't have anyone getting in the way of that. Am I clear?"

My husband was home and all I wanted to do was be up under him despite his weirdness. Instead, I was sitting on the edge of my mother's tub looking down at her naked body. As she sat in murky water, I couldn't understand why at this age she had a busted lip. When you're as old as her, what are you fighting for? Dry blood rested on her right shoulder and when I first saw her, I thought I would pass out.

Ever since Grainger went missing, she tumbled downhill. Even harder. My mother was never good at housekeeping but now her place was atrocious. Dead mice were scattered throughout the living room due to the spoiled food she left everywhere and all of her clothes were so filthy they smelled like steamed shit. When I asked what she wore daily, she said she would pick the least dirty outfit.

"What about panties, ma? How do you find anything here?"

"I had the same ones on three weeks in a row. I just wash them out in the sink." She pointed at the floor.

When I looked down at the ones she took off, a brown stain ran in the middle of the cream panties that were once white. I could feel my stomach rolling in disgust.

"Ma, what are you doing with yourself?" I asked as tears streamed down my face. "Look at how you're living!" I paused. "Why haven't you called me?"

"Because I was angry!"

"At me?" I asked touching her shoulder. "Why?"

"I don't know." She shrugged before sighing. "With Grainger missing and my granddaughter dead, I just...I guess I just wanted to be alone."

There she goes making everything about her. Jasmine was my baby, not hers.

I wiped my hand down my face. "Who hit you?" I asked changing the subject.

"My boyfriend Chris."

"But I thought you were dealing with some nigga name Edwin?"

"No, Denim. You don't remember anything I say. I was dating Edwin but then I got with his cousin Chris. Remember?"

I didn't.

She leaned back in the tub and grabbed a washcloth. "Chris thought I was back with Edwin again and he beat me 'cause he was jealous." She smiled. "I don't know why men always fight over me."

She sounded dumb.

"You talking about Chris the drunk who be hanging out front of Handles liquor store?" I frowned.

"Yeah."

When I thought about how stank that man was, I wanted to vomit again. My mother let anybody with a dick run up in her. She didn't give a fuck if it was clean, dirty or had sores. She had zero standards. "Forget all that shit. Ma, why does this house look like this?"

"Because I haven't had a chance to clean it." She pointed to some wrinkled white papers with my sister's face on them that were sitting on the top of the toilet. "I've been trying to find my baby," she sobbed. "I just gotta find her, Denim. Just thinking about Grainger being out there without me drives me mad. I know something happened to her. I can feel it!"

My heart was broken because although my mother could be annoying at times, there wasn't anything I wouldn't do for her. I bought her the house that she ruined. I hired a maid to come over weekly even though she was never home to let her inside. I paid for her gastric bypass surgery and she even lost a lot of her excess weight, only to put most of it back on.

Still, she never gave a fuck about me.

It was always about Grainger.

I knew she was close to Grainger. Closer than she was to me. It was evident when I married Bradley, who my sister used to date. My mother blamed me for hurting Grainger's feelings even though their relationship was over way before we got together. But now I really knew that she loved Grainger more than me. She never asked me how I was doing now that my daughter was dead or while my husband was in jail. It was always about my sister even with her being gone.

"Mama, I hired some boys to put the posters up around the city. Why aren't you letting them do it? You don't have to worry about this type of shit."

"Because I don't trust them," she wept harder. "They probably just take the posters and put them in the trash."

"But I saw them around the city, ma. They are doing it."

"I still don't trust them!" she yelled. "And where were you, Denim? I was calling you all day and you didn't answer the phone."

"Bradley's home from jail," I sighed. "I went to get him today. I left you a message telling you that."

Instead of being happy for me, she lowered her head. Her face spread into a frown and I felt as if she was about to hit me. "I don't like that mothafucka, Denim. I been telling you that any man who would lay up with your sister and then you is not a man. I wish you would listen to me."

She sounded ridiculous. "Ma, how can you say some shit like that when you live in squalor?" I yelled. "I mean look at this fucking house! I couldn't even get to the bathroom without tripping three times. And the smell in this bitch makes my stomach turn, ma. So please don't tell me about laying up with a man because at least mine is clean!"

"That may be true," she said nodding her head. "But I know a bum when I see one. And that man of yours has something to do with Grainger being missing. I don't care what he says."

"Ma, please stop the weak shit," I responded trying not to hate my mother for disrespecting my husband. "He was really concerned when he found out she was missing and still is. He asks me every day if I heard anything about where she may be."

"Is that why he raped her?"

"Mama, I'm not about to sit in this filth and talk about my husband." The only thing on my mind was getting out of that house and rolling up a blunt once I got in my car. "You can have your opinions but at the end of the day I'm gonna always be a Kennedy and it's time for you to get used to it."

Silence.

"I don't have Grainger anymore, Denim," she whispered. "And I need you. I'm all alone." She placed her hand on her left breast. "Don't forget about that while you're living in paradise with the husband you would give up everything for."

"What does that mean, mama?"

"That I need to move with you. Or I might kill myself."

I was sitting in the car smoking a blunt outside of my mother's house. I couldn't see letting her live with me but what else was I going to do? I believed her wholeheartedly when she said she would kill herself and I couldn't let that happen.

After taking a deep pull, I tapped my blunt into the ashtray and called Race. The moment she picked up the phone, I could hear cheering in the background. I guess the family was celebrating already. "What up, sis?" she said. "Where you at? We trying to party with Bradley, and all he keep talking about is you."

I smiled. At least he was thinking of me. "I'll be there in a second. You know funky Chris?"

"The nigga who be hanging on our most profitable block in D.C.?" she giggled. "Who tried to rob Jamaican Wayne and got his face fractured in 21 places with his fake gun?" she giggled.

"Yeah," I said pulling on my blunt before releasing clouds of smoke into the ceiling.

"I know his dusty ass. Why? What's up?"

"I want you to find someone to make him comfortable," I said, which was code for kill that nigga.

"Say no more. You already know what it is."

CHAPTER TWO
THE RUSSIANS

*I*akov and Arkadi Lenin sat at the ends of the table where three other bosses were also seated. The painted red bricks on the wall appeared to be on fire as the sun shined through the huge oval windows of one of the Lenins' many hideouts. Every last one of the men invited was powerful in his own right and they ruled the most lucrative drug businesses around the country.

A large glass jug of thick red liquid sat in the middle of the table. Each attendee, with the exception of the Russians, wondered what it was.

In the corner sat Mellvue, Arkadi's devoted fiancé. Most of her heart shaped face was covered by large brown Tom Ford glasses to disguise the blackened eye her fiancé blessed her with earlier in the week. Although scarred, Mellvue, a full-bred Russian, was both beautiful and intimidating at the same time.

Seated at the table was Vito Gambino of the Gambino Family, an Italian mob syndicate out of New York. Most of his facial features were unassuming except for his eyes. They were large and cold—the folds of wrinkles on his dark skin acted like open curtains surrounding them. He and his family killed many and they often broke code to seal their seat at the multimillion-dollar operation.

Next to him was Derrick Reaper from New Jersey. Although his money came from the drug business, his value lay in his access to soldiers. Under his command he possessed one hundred armed hoodlums who were affectionately called the Reapers. Although they were all cold-blooded, his biggest threat was Larry who had a reputation for killing his enemies and their loved ones no matter where they were, even in church.

A thug from birth, you'd never know it to look at Derrick's features. His dark chocolate skin was smooth and flawless. In fact, the only distinguishing mark on his face was a black mole that sat ever so slightly under his left eye. It was said that he loved to kill with his hands so much that he kept them clasped in front of him, even at the moment, to prevent the urge to snuff out life.

Across from Derrick was Jim Rabiu, an African from California. He dominated the west coast in both muscle and cocaine. He was a womanizer who often used females for sexual gratification before putting them in servitude. In his personal life, he was a monster but in business, he made many hopeful dealers millionaires. So he was respected and revered by the vilest on the streets.

Unlike most Africans, his light skin, courtesy of his white father and black mother, was scarred from all of the knives taken to his face as a teenager by jealous villagers in the hopes of dismantling his looks. They were successful in their attempt because at the moment, he was a horrid sight to behold.

"I guess I'll ask first," Vito said as he ran a toothpick through the meat in his teeth. "What's up with the red jar?"

Arkadi grinned. "It contains drop of blood from every man we've ever killed and soon it will contain blood of our latest enemy."

Vito shook his head and tossed the soiled toothpick on the table. He leaned back in his chair and rested his hands on his large belly. "Well, let's get on with it. Why are we here?"

"You're here because I make you very rich men," Arkadi responded as his piercing blue eyes stared at him across the table. His Russian accent both thick and strong. "Isn't that what you want?"

"First off, I'm already rich," he clarified. "And what I want and what it will cost me is another thing entirely."

Iakov, the youngest of the Russian brothers, took a sip of his favorite vodka, which he never left home without. "We know whereabouts of powerful man," he said. "A man with purest cocaine you ever come in contact with in life."

"So what's your dilemma?" Derrick asked.

"We can't get to him alone," Iakov said plainly. "And that's problem."

"So if you get this man, how does that benefit us?" Jim responded.

"If we have access to him, that means you do, too," Arkadi replied. "This is win-win situation for everybody."

Vito laughed. "Stop the games, Arkadi. You and I both know that there's no such thing as something for nothing."

"You're right," he admitted. "In order to bring this man in, we need your help. At moment, he is in the custody of a very powerful family. But the streets don't know he's been kidnapped because he's still able to run business. Now if we can bring him in it means we'll have access to his cocaine."

"So basically he's a golden goose," Derrick responded.

"Not only that, this man has access to worldwide distribution methods," Iakov said. "Due to a charity organization he runs, he owns planes and can fly across world without being inspected by government. We need this man for both his cocaine and his power."

"If you get him, what makes you think he'll work for you?" Derrick asked.

"We'll put him in position where he has no choice," Arkadi responded.

"So which family has him?" Derrick questioned.

Iakov hit the edge of a cigarette pack on the side of his finger. Removing one, he lit it with the gold lighter in his pocket. "Kennedy Kings have him," he responded before blowing a cloud of smoke into the air.

Upon hearing Kennedy, the men moved around uneasily in their seats. As with all powerful drug empires of the time, they were fully aware of the clout the Kennedy Kings possessed. Although murder didn't follow the Kennedy brand during the earlier years of their business, when their wives took over the operation during a period when the men were missing, all that changed.

"I'm sixty-two years old," Vito explained. "And I have more money than I know what to do with. On top of that, murder within my organization has decreased one percent a year due to the understanding I have with people in and out of my operation." He pointed a stiff finger into the table. "If I get into a war with the Kennedy Kings, that will change." He unbuttoned the collared white shirt he was wearing under his blue blazer, exposing vines of thick black hair. "Now I'm not opposed to going to war but it has to be worth the risks. And I don't hear the benefits yet."

"I feel the same," Jim responded. "Things are going smooth and I'd like to keep it that way."

"If you help, I'll offer you a thirty percent reduction per kilo," Arkadi said. "Much better than what you're getting from your current suppliers, yes?"

"Is that good enough reason?" Iakov asked arrogantly.

Vito and Jim were definitely impressed but drugs were not Derrick's specialty. Judging by their expressions they were pleased but he needed more convincing. "Unfortunately for you, I don't sell coke," Derrick advised. "My first question is what do you need from me?"

"We need men," Iakov paused, "from all of you, which is why you're here. There is going to be war and we need available soldiers who can help us infiltrate Kennedy King operation. Your Reapers could do that for us, yes?"

"What's in it for me?"

"For the use of your men, we will pay you one million dollars," Arkadi responded. "Plus expenses."

Derrick slammed his hands together and ran his tongue over his lips. "Me and my crew can work with that."

"So what is your plan?" Vito asked.

"First, we combine forces, take down the Kennedy King organization and smoke Mitch out," Iakov responded. "Once we have him, we give him ultimatum he can't refuse. Work with us directly or die a harsh death." He touched the top of the bloody jar.

"Derrick, do you have anyone who can move with precision?"

Derrick rubbed his hands together and licked his lips. "I have a killer with zero compassion. He would kill me if I failed to pay him enough."

Iakov smiled. "Who is this man?"

"His name is Larry."

Iakov laughed. "A simple name for such ruthless killer."

Derrick nodded in agreement and asked, "So when do you want to start?"

"Why put murder off a day when you can do it tonight?"

CHAPTER THREE
BAMBI

Our bedroom seemed chilly and I wasn't sure if it was the temperature or the fact that Kevin and I were still beefing.

I lay on my side of the bed with my back faced my husband. He was on the other side looking away from me. Since our beef, this was how we slept every night.

A pillow was stuffed between my legs and I was so horny I was about to rub one out on the edge of it. As bad as I wanted some dick, I was not about to kiss his ass either. At least that's what I told myself.

There was a reason for our beef.

A few years back, I thought Kevin, Bradley, Camp and Ramirez were dead after being on a video call with Kevin, only to see gunfire break out behind him. The screen went black and he was gone. Kevin and his brothers went missing for months and although I was going to kill my husband, due to him cheating on me prior to the serial killer coming into the establishment, when I realized how it felt for him to be out of my life I was devastated.

But things still needed to be taken care of on the home front with them gone so I had to step up. My husband and his brothers were bosses and a big drug deal with the Russians needed to take place despite their absence, or we wouldn't be able to take care of ourselves.

We needed the money. So I convinced my sisters to pose as our husbands to meet the Russians and make the cocaine drop.

Even though the Russians knew that we were not our husbands and nicknamed us Pretty Kings, the deal went through. But it almost didn't. All because Kevin's aunt Bunny was trying to steal the cocaine needed for the delivery. If she had been successful in her attempt, it would've set my family back financially.

So I killed her.

I almost got away with it but Kevin's cousin Cloud found something I left at Bunny's house during the murder. It was a Band-Aid that fell off the scar I had it on. My DNA was all over it. I was so careless when normally I wasn't. If the cops would've found it they would've arrested me for her murder.

Instead of keeping my secret, Cloud, who always wanted to fuck me, blackmailed me into a sexual relationship. But I couldn't take it anymore. His touch, his kisses all made me want to throw up. So I told my husband everything, including the fact that I killed Bunny. Kevin was devastated.

First, he instructed me to kill Cloud for his betrayal and he vowed to kill me the moment our twin sons turned 21.

Although that was a few years away, I always wondered if he would make good on that threat.

Trying to drive him sexually insane like he was making me, I yawned and scooted my butt a little closer to him. I was naked from the waist down so I was hoping it would work. When I couldn't feel his skin I yawned and scooted even closer. Now my ass was directly on his cotton boxers.

My heart was beating rapidly because this was the first time I made a move for Kevin.

"What you doing, Bambi?" he said in a heavy bass voice.

My body tensed up and I didn't respond. It was already embarrassing trying to get him to touch me. The last thing I wanted was to admit to being awake. So I remained silent and closed my eyes tighter.

I heard him say, "I know what you...I know you fucking with me." His voice was low and I had a feeling my seduction was working. "I'm not going for it, Bambi."

Instead of responding, I yawned and moved closer into him. "Did you say something?" I asked in a heavy voice as if I was asleep.

"Fuck," he said under his breath as if he were trying to hold back. The room was pitch black but I could feel his tension. I knew for a fact that his dick was probably growing with anticipation. "Bambi, get your ass off me."

I remained silent again.

"Bambi, move!" he yelled.

I stayed where I was and popped one of my cheeks before yawning again.

"Fuck this shit," he said.

Before I knew it, the bed rattled and he was rising up. He stood over top of me and gripped my arm, forcing me on my back. I looked up into the whites of his eyes as he pushed my legs roughly apart. I grinned inside when I saw his dick was already stiff. I could feel the juice of my pussy ease toward the bed and suddenly he was inside of me.

Horny, I wrapped my arms around him and I could feel him exhale. Like all of the tension we had for each other was released. The sensation coursing through my body drove me insane as he continually pounded my pussy. He was still working for his nut but I came already.

Still enjoying my fuck massage, he leaned down. His chest pressed against my breasts and he slid his arm behind my neck and pulled it close to his lips as he continued to move inside of me. "Why you playing games with me, bitch?" he asked, getting rougher. "You know I don't fuck with you. Don't you?"

Kevin was talking a bunch of shit and I was paying him no mind. He wanted this pussy as much as I wanted him. Since he was still on top of me, I decided to cum enough to last me through the drought. Besides, I wasn't sure when or if we would do this again. So trying to get mine off once more, I bucked my hips wildly. Then I ran my nails down his back and he moaned louder.

I knew his hot spots.

Every last one of them.

"So my cousin was in this pussy too, huh?" he said angrily as he gripped my ass cheeks and pulled as if he were trying to separate them. "You let him fuck you, bitch? I should kill you."

I could tell he was mad but the anger in his voice was doing nothing but making my pussy wetter. I remained quiet and before I knew it, he moaned out harshly and came inside of me.

Before getting off my body, he remained on top of me for a few seconds. His chest rose and fell heavily into mine. "This doesn't change anything, Bambi. I don't care how good this pussy is."

"I didn't think it would," I responded. "Now get the fuck off me. You too sweaty."

Fully satisfied, I was about to roll over and go to sleep when Race busted in our bedroom without knocking. "We got a family emergency," she said anxiously. "The Russians just attacked!"

My husband, brothers-in-law and sisters-in-law were sitting around the large table in our dining room. Although the compound was new, I was having the finishing touches placed on a secret bunker in Virginia that was off the grid. It was big enough to comfortably sleep sixty people. I had it created because I predicted that there would come a time when the beef with the Russians would reach a new high and we wouldn't be able to stay here.

Now was that time.

Before beginning the meeting, I was waiting for Kevin to get off the phone. He was talking to our sons Melo and Noah who were in college in Arizona. We wanted them as far away from everything we had going on as possible. So we shipped them out as much as we could and I had a feeling they resented us for it.

When he ended the call he walked over to the table and said, "They're okay." He stuffed the phone in his pocket.

"Did they ask about me?" I questioned.

"Melo did but Noah...well...you know." He sat down.

My family looked at me with pity because they knew what we all did, that one of my sons hated me. And no matter what I did to show Noah I loved him just as much as Melo, it didn't work.

I took a deep breath and said, "Race, give us the update."

"I just got a call from Sarge," she said as she ran her hands through her brown hair. "He told me the Russians took over three of our blocks and killed fifteen soldiers. But they used Larry from the Reapers to do it. I don't know when they got up with this dude but we have to put him out of his misery soon.

He's vile, Bambi. And I'm not opposed to getting him in the basement of one of our buildings and torturing his ass if need be." If Race was down for one thing, maiming and torturing was it.

"I can't believe this shit!" Ramirez yelled slamming a closed fist on the table. "I thought the nigga Larry was locked up! When his bitch ass get out?"

"I don't know but he's home now," Race sighed. "And now he's with the Russians and attacking our operation."

"Sounds like it's time for war to me," Ramirez said rubbing his hands together.

"Nigga, you always want war," Camp said. "Let's sort things out before we jump out there."

Ramirez shook his head. "Brother, there's nothing to sort out. It's time to attack."

"I'm cool with a war if need be but how much is this shit going to cost us?" Bradley added to the matter. "We're already tapping at the walls due to the bunker Bambi's building."

"A bunker that will save our lives," I explained. He made it sound irrelevant and I had to check his ass. "A bunker worthy of kings."

Kevin sighed. "Did you get word to our other men, Race?" Kevin asked as he crossed his arms over his chest. "If not, we need to do that right now. We can't deal with any more casualties. With our soldiers or their families."

"I did that before I came to get you guys," she responded. "All of our men are off the blocks and in for the night until we can figure this shit out."

I stood up and leaned against the cool wall. Slowly I looked at my family and exhaled. "This is it," I said softly. "This is the event we knew was going to happen. The only thing we didn't know was when." I stuffed my hands into my green fatigues. "We have to meet with the east coast bosses. The ones that Mitch works with directly."

"Why?" Kevin frowned.

"Because we need their help."

"Need their help for what?" Denim questioned. She was sitting on Bradley's lap and his hand rested on her thigh. They both were smoking on a blunt making it cloudy in the room. "We have enough men to take care of two white Russians."

"She's right," Bradley added. "If we give the proper word we can have them killed by the end of the night."

"We're not dealing with a couple of hood niggas from down south," I said seriously. "We're dealing with two enemies who have worldwide connections. What we need is more manpower and a specialized killer to get at Larry's bitch ass. If we don't get him now he will continue to pick off our men."

"You preaching to the choir," Ramirez said. "The question is who do we get for a job like this?"

"We need someone who isn't affiliated with anybody, who we can use solely for our benefit. Who's smart enough to move around the Russians and take out Larry. If we don't cut him off at the legs now he'll just be getting started on us."

"Have anybody in mind?" Race asked.

I looked around at everyone again. "Yes. Do you remember the person who was going around Baltimore robbing and killing niggas for sport?"

"I remember hearing about that shit," Kevin said scratching his head. "But nobody ever saw that dude."

"Yeah, the only thing they knew was that he was tall and had green eyes," Ramirez said as he sipped a cup of coffee.

"Didn't they call the nigga Goon?" Camp asked as he knocked a few cookie crumbs off the t-shirt with his missing son on it.

There was a lot of crazy shit going on in our family. Including the fact that Scarlett gave their son up to a couple and told Camp that he was kidnapped. I was the only one in the family outside of Scarlett who knew where he was.

"What makes you think Goon is a man?" I asked Camp.

All of the men laughed. "Let's see, because they said slim was tall and had green eyes I think."

"So everybody tall with green eyes is a man?" I asked trying to suppress my laughter. "Brother, you sound stupid."

Silence.

"Well what makes you think it's a woman?" Kevin asked.

I walked over to him and sat on the edge of the table. My pussy was still full of his cum. I looked down at him and said, "Because only a woman could kill, go into hiding and not say a word. Men feel the need to brag on such frivolous things. We don't."

Sarah walked into the dining room and said, "What's this about?" She put her hands on her growing hips and looked down at Denim. "Why didn't you tell your mother there was a meeting?"

This bitch right here...

"Mama, now is not the time we are talking about something—"

"I know, very important," she said rubbing her big belly while finishing Denim's sentence.

I loved Denim with all of my heart but I hated her fucking mother.

"Ma, please come back later," Denim begged. "This is really private."

Sarah looked at Denim and then at me. Staring directly into my eyes, she said, "I know, I know, this is business. Then again, it always is." She blew a kiss my way and walked out.

When she disappeared I asked, "How long is she going to be here?"

"I'm working to find her a crib now," Denim said rubbing her hands down her face. "But let's get into all that later. We're losing track of what's really important."

"So what we gonna do, Bambi?" Scarlett asked looking into my eyes. Her red hair hung over her white face and partially covered her eyes. I could tell that just like me, she was probably preparing for sleep before she got the call that we'd been hit.

Although she was talking to me, Kevin answered. I always got the impression that he resented me when it came to war talk and it fucked my head up. "For now, me and Bambi gonna go upstairs and talk to Mitch in the attic," Kevin said. "To see what he thinks about all of this."

"And after that, I'll try to set a meeting up with the east coast bosses to see if we can count on their support. Although I won't lie, they don't see the Russians' actions as a threat to their businesses right now."

"So how you gonna get them to change their minds?" Scarlett asked.

"I got a plan or two. But for now I'll keep it down to a simple conversation." I looked over at Race before saying anything else.

Lately she'd been consumed with pity over a chick she and Ramirez was fucking whom I believed she killed. She would hang out at the strip club and I was starting to wonder if I could trust her to handle business. Still, when it came to the soldiers in our organization, she and Sarge were the go-to people. They knew everybody who murdered for us well.

"Race, I need you to find me a specialized killer. Can you handle it?"

"I got you, Bambi. I won't let you down."

Kevin and I walked upstairs and toward the first corridor. We nodded at the two armed soldiers who protected Mitch's door at all times even though he was in our house. They were there for two reasons. To keep him inside and if there was a war, to keep the intruders out.

Mitch wasn't some white boy with a little clout. He was the sole reason we were at war with the Russians. He was the most important component to our operation.

He was the connect.

He manufactured the purest cocaine in Mexico. He supplied most of the east coast and a few states down south and the Russians wanted him.

In their greed, they plotted to kidnap him and force him into a business relationship. But we found out about it and beat them to it. Using one of Mitch's private planes, we snuck him out of his home in Mexico by hiding him inside a designer wooden table. We got him and his wife Amber away minutes before the Russians arrived at his house. His son was shipped to Arizona to stay with an aunt. And the same team we had looking out for our twins, we had watching his son too.

With Mitch in our possession, we were able to control the distribution. Our business didn't suffer one bit, but the Russians' business did. We cut them off all supply, forcing them to spend more money on a lesser quality product.

We realized the current situation that Mitch lived in was temporary but he resented us. Instead of feeling like a guest in a room that resembled a five star hotel suite, he felt like a prisoner. He wanted to be out on the beach with his beautiful wife. I didn't blame him. But until we rid the world of the Russians, we couldn't take any chances.

He had to stay here.

When we walked through the door of his suite I saw his wife Amber was taking a nap on a white fur comforter. Every time I saw her, I knew immediately why he chose her to be his wife. The configuration of her body was long and symmetrical. And even while asleep, her physique fell into an elegant pose. Her pale legs dangled off of the edge of the bed and her brown hair spread against the white sheet. She looked picture perfect.

"What can I do for you?" Mitch asked. His back was faced us and he focused on the screen TV on the wall. He was watching the movie *The Color Purple*. I guess he was thinking of a time when white people owned blacks.

I laughed to myself.

Times have changed, white boy.

"It's about the Russians," Kevin said. "They just took out fifteen of our men. We figure many more will follow."

Mitch shook his head but remained looking at the TV. "What do you want me to do? I'm the Golden Goose, remember? The only job I have is to make phone calls to keep the pipelines to the distribution line open." He laughed. "It's all about the coke and money."

42   By T. Styles

"Mitch, you know it ain't like that. My wife brought you here to protect you." He paused. "You're family and I know it feels like prison but it's for your own good."

"Then why can't I roam the house? Why must I stay in this room?"

Silence.

"Because you don't understand what we're doing by bringing you here," I said. "If we thought you did, we would offer you that luxury. But we're afraid you'll leave and get yourself killed. And I can't have that. Not now."

He sat the remote down and walked over to me as if he wanted to hurt me. But Kevin pushed him back. "That's close enough," Kevin said.

Mitch removed the glare from his face and said, "I wasn't going to hurt her. I just wanted to...I just wanted to talk to her." He looked me in my eyes and I could tell he despised me.

"I don't care if you were or not," Kevin said. "With the glare you got in your stare, I would feel more comfortable if you stayed away from my wife."

Surprised that Kevin took up for me, I looked over at him. Kevin's eyes met mine for a second before he looked away. I guess he hated that he was taking up for me since he supposedly hated me so much.

"Mitch, this is not a punishment," I said after running my fingers through my hair. "I mean, look at how you live. You have your own chef, the finest wines and anything else you desire."

"Except my freedom."

"Heavy is the head that supplies the coke," I said. "You know that."

He lowered his head. "What do you want?" He looked at Kevin and then back at me. "What do you want from your Golden Goose now?"

"Do you have any men who could support us if things kicked off in this war with the Russians?" Kevin asked.

He sighed. "How many do you need?"

"About one hundred," I responded.

He laughed. "I don't have that sort of manpower in the States."

I knew he was lying.

"If we were in Mexico things would be different," he continued.

"But we aren't in Mexico," Kevin responded. "We're right here and I need your help."

"My problem and your problem exactly." He paused. "I don't know how this is going to end up but I have a suggestion that might save us a lot of time and bloodshed."

"What's that?" Kevin asked.

"Let me work directly with the Russians. I'll cut you in a percent of all of the business I do with them. With that agreement, they will be satisfied and you will be too. It will end this crazy war and allow me to go home with my wife. Where we belong."

I ran my finger down the protruding scar on my face. "Do you see this shit?" I said stepping closer to Mitch. "I got this from a blade the Russians slid across my face."

"I know," he said under his breath.

"Do you really, mothafucka?" I yelled. "Because if my memory serves me correctly, I earned this when I refused to tell them where you were. If I hadn't, you may be dead or in prison." I put my finger in his face. "I'm sick of you playing the martyr, Mitch. And I suggest you start showing me a little more respect around here." I snapped my fingers and the two armed men outside of the door aimed their barrels at his head. "Because the conditions here can change in an instant if I so desire."

CHAPTER FOUR
RACE

The bed felt comfortable as I lay on my back, trying to take a nap. After the late night meeting I was exhausted. I felt myself about to drift off to sleep when suddenly the door to my room opened and I knew it was Ramirez.

I didn't feel like talking to him about why our marriage would not work so I kept my eyes closed.

When I felt the sheet slide off my body I couldn't believe what he was trying to do. Have sex. We hadn't fucked since before Carey was killed so why was he coming at me now?

When the weight of his body lowered the mattress slightly, my heartbeat quickened. I just knew he was going to try to fuck me. Instead, he pushed my legs apart and lifted my nightgown.

Within seconds, he was lapping at my pussy, hitting my clit softly and repeatedly. In that moment, I hated myself. Not because he was touching me without permission, but because it felt so good.

I was a tough bitch but the hardest thing I ever did was remain stiff, with my eyes closed while he caused my body to experience all kinds of ecstasy. Instead of faking like I was asleep, I wanted to cheer him on and say, "Right there, Ramirez. Keep it like that. It feels so good."

Instead, I lay still with my eyes closed and did everything I could to prevent him from knowing that I reached an orgasm. He licked at me for two more minutes after I came and I thought I was losing my mind because it tickled and my clit was sensitive.

When he was done he walked back toward the door and whispered, "I love you, Race. And I'm not going to stop fighting for you." He walked out.

The next day I was livid about him fucking up my head by eating me out. I wanted him to know that no matter what he did the night before, we were still over.

My soon to be ex-husband was standing in the middle of our bedroom looking at the divorce papers I had drawn up a week ago. The pen to sign them and get this shit over with was in his other hand.

Why wouldn't he use it to scribble his signature down?

Part of me wanted it done with. Wanted him to let me walk out. But the other part of me was scared to be alone. Who was I if I wasn't Ramirez's wife? Would I even still be a Kennedy?

He flipped to the last sheet, laughed and tossed the papers on the bed. His lips tightened and he said through clenched teeth, "I'm not signing that shit, Race. You my wife now and you're going to stay my fucking wife. For as long as I have breath in my body. And as long as you have breath in yours."

I stomped over to the dresser and slammed my fist on it. The half bottle of Hennessey that I had been nursing all morning wobbled and I picked it up, took a swig and slammed it back down. Angry, I turned around to face him. "You said you would do it, Ramirez. You promised to let me go. What's different now?"

"Because you don't really want a divorce, baby," he said holding one hand over his chest. "If you did, you wouldn't still be here. Don't do this shit to me! I'm begging you."

I walked up to him with my arms crossed over my chest, afraid of what I might do to him. Real slowly I parted my lips and said, "I been telling you I want a divorce for months and now is the time." I paused. "And like I told you in the past, only reason I'm still here is because I haven't found the right place. The moment I get the house of my dreams, I'm gone and you need to prepare yourself for that."

"Do you even get what's going on right now? We at war, Race! Fuck I look like divorcing you at a time like this?" He gripped my shoulders and pulled me toward him. Gazing down at me, he said, "Not over no stripper we both brought into our marriage."

I wiggled out of his grasp. "You don't get it, do you?" I asked angrily. "It's not about us fucking a bitch together. It's about you falling in love with her."

"And you didn't fall in love with her?" He paused. "Keep it one hundred, Race! You talked to her more than I did. And don't tell me I didn't hear you crying over her a few times in the bathroom when you thought I wasn't listening," he continued. "You miss her, baby, but I'm over the chick. I understand why you had to lay the murder game down and all I want right now is my wife back!"

"You should've understood that the moment I put a bullet in her head instead of acting like your wife was dead as opposed to your side bitch."

I felt myself wanting to cry but I sucked it in. Ramirez violated by catching feelings and I hated him for it. I hated him for making me kill her because I knew in my heart that she was perfect...for both of us.

48   By T. Styles

I turned around and faced the door when I heard someone in our room. "Excuse me, I don't mean to interrupt, but do you know where my daughter is?" Sarah asked hanging in the doorway.

I gasped when I saw what this bitch had on. She was wearing a sheer red nightgown and I wanted to smack the shit out of her because you could see every line on her body. Her large saggy breasts, her hairy pussy and the tiger striped stretch marks on her legs and belly. I knew she was going to be a problem when Denim said she had to stay with us but I never expected no shit like this.

"Sarah, if you don't get the fuck up out my room with that shit on I'ma lay hands on you," I promised.

Sarah's eyes widened and she laughed before raising a wine glass she was carrying to her lips. The red liquid splashed against her mouth and she stretched her tongue into the glass. When she was done with her stinky, supposed-to-be-erotic sip, she lowered her glass and looked over my head at Ramirez.

"Why you mad, cutie?" she said to me with eyes still on him. "Is it because you're afraid that that fine ass man candy of yours will want some of this good pussy?" She raised her nightgown like she was about to flash him and I lifted my red tank top, showing the handle of my Beretta in my jeans.

The stupid smile vanished from her face. "No need to be so antsy." She looked into my eyes and back at my gun handle. "I was just searching for Denim. Since she ain't here, I guess I'll check around the rest of the house."

"You go do that," I said.

"I will. But you're going to wish you didn't unveil your gun to me. I promise you that."

When she left I turned around and looked at Ramirez. He had his hand over his mouth like he was trying to suppress a laugh. When I saw his face turning red, I busted out laughing too. Before I knew it, he was on the floor in tears and I was on the bed.

Together we had the kind of laugh that made me forget all about my troubles and it took both of us a minute to simmer down. When I was done he crawled up on the bed next to me and said, "You see, baby? We still got a lot of love left. Don't end us." He grabbed my hand and kissed the top of it. "I'm begging you."

CHAPTER FIVE
DENIM

I was putting on my jacket, about to go with Bambi to get my toes done, when Bradley opened the bathroom door. Steam flowed around the silhouette of his body as if he was submerged in fog. Instantly my pussy moistened as I took in his sexy body. "Where you going, baby?"

"About to get a pedicure with Bambi." I zipped up my jacket and walked over to the dresser to slide some lipstick on.

He strolled out the doorway and walked up behind me. Pressing his damp body against my back, he raised my blue dreads and kissed me on the neck. "Don't go out tonight," he whispered before sucking the bottom of my ear. "I copped a fresh bag of kush from my man. Let's put paper planes in the air and fuck all night."

I grinned and said, "I can't mess with you today, Bradley. We been going at it non-stop. I have to spend time with my sister at—"

He pushed away from me and his nostrils flared. His lips parted like he was about to tell me something before closing again. "You fucking Bambi or something? You into that dyke shit like Race? Huh?"

The comment was so out of left field that it took the breath out of me. I dropped the lipstick, turned around and walked over to him. When I was an arm's length away from him, I smacked the shit out of him.

Hard.

Pointing a stiff finger at him, I said, "If you ever say some shit like that to me again I'll..."

"You'll do what, Denim?" he chuckled. "Leave me?"

Silence.

"Because I'd like to see you try, bitch," he continued, walking into the bathroom and slamming the door behind him.

What did they do to my husband in that prison? He wasn't the same since he'd been back. Or maybe he was always this man but I didn't know until now.

I told Bambi I wasn't in the mood to go get a pedicure. Bradley's possessiveness had me feeling like I was doing something wrong. Like I was neglecting him for going out and I needed to get my mind together to figure out how I was going to handle this. He seemed obsessed and it was so unlike him.

We always trusted each other.

Was he guilty of something and trying to turn it on me?

Instead of going with Bambi, I went to one of the guest rooms down in the west wing of the bunker and rolled up a blunt. I finished that one and was just about to roll another when I saw my mother walking down the hallway in a freak outfit that raised the hair all over my body.

This is the type of shit I was talking about. Behavior like this was the main reason we didn't have a close relationship. Instead of being the fifty-something year-old woman that she was, she was gallivanting around this bitch in whore outfits. She was probably hoping to get some dick from one of my sisters' husbands.

It was hard enough for me to convince them to let her stay. But after she interrupted the meeting the other day, I doubted she'd be able to hang around here long.

I put my blunt in the ashtray, hopped off the bed and ran out of the room to catch her. Walking up behind her, I took another look at what she was wearing and shook my head. "Ma, what the fuck do you have on? Why you didn't put on the sweatpants I bought you last week?"

She swayed from side to side before looking back at me. Leaning on the banister for support, she said, "If I want to wear a comforter I'll slide it off my bed." She paused. "I mean what the fuck is wrong with you jealous ass bitches around here? If ya'll chose to dress half as sexy as I do, instead of toting your big guns around like dykes, you might be able to get some dick."

"Mama!" I yelled.

"Mama, shit! It ain't my fault ya'll niggas can't keep their eyes off me," she responded, her words slurring around in her mouth.

I shook my body, trying to get some of the disgust I had for her off my skin. "You can't stay here dressed like that. You just can't. If you want to live in this house you will be dressed properly at all times." I paused. "Don't make me regret my decision to let you live here until your house get's done."

Her eyes widened and I could see them glossing over like she was about to cry. "You just want me gone in case I find out something. Is that it?" she asked with a glob of spit oozing down the side of her mouth.

She was drunk and I had enough.

I snatched the empty wine glass from her. "You don't know what you talking about." I gripped her arm and ushered her toward her room. "Come on."

"What happened to Grainger?" she screamed. "What happened to my baby?"

"She's probably with some crackhead, ma," I responded. "She was never an angel. You know that."

I pulled her again and she tried to fight me but she was too drunk to get away. In the end, she was in the room we set up for her and I walked her over to the bed. She must've been tired because she crawled under the sheets without a fight and I sat the glass down on the table next to her before flopping on the edge of the mattress.

I looked over at her and wiped her graying hair out of her face. She looked sad, pitiful even, and the guilt of how I was treating her weighed on my head. Tucking a few strands of her hair behind her ear, I said, "Mama, I love you and I don't mean to be mean. I just want you to know that I'm not the enemy. I never will be."

"Baby, is everything okay?" Bradley asked walking into the room.

Sometimes, during the tough moments, I forgot he was home. But when he popped up like he did now, I realized I wasn't alone anymore.

"Yeah, I was just—"

"What did you do with my daughter?" my mother screamed suddenly, causing me to leap up. "I know you did something to her, Bradley! Where is she?"

His eyebrows pulled together tightly. "Sarah, like I told you the last million times you asked, I didn't do anything to her or with her. I need you to stop with the accusations because you causing problems between me and my wife."

"Liar! I know you did something to my child," she yelled louder. "And when I find out what, I'm going to—"

"Do what?" he yelled stepping deeper into the bedroom. "You not gonna do shit because everything you have, everything you eat, and all the whore outfits you sport around this joint are courtesy of me. Without my money, you'd be out on the streets. Keep talking shit and I'll show you how the broke really live."

Hearing how he was talking to my mother got me heated. I walked toward him and said, "Hold up, baby. My mother didn't mean it like that. She's drunk and—"

"Why you always take up for her?" he paused. "I'm sick of you letting her come into your life and dictate how and when you do shit, Denim. She shouldn't be here! She had her chance at a life and she fucked it up. Don't let her ruin yours too because you refuse to obey your husband!"

"Bradley," I yelled. "Why are you acting so different lately?" I paused. "Regardless of how you feel, she's still my fucking mother!" I screamed.

I could see the anger wash away from his face. In its place was disappointment. He curled his hands into fists before relaxing them. "I came in here to apologize for calling you a bitch. But if we don't work out, it'll be because of her. I want you to remember that." He pointed at my mother and stormed out.

I watched him walk away but my stare was still on the door long after he left. I heard my mother calling me but I didn't look at her. I couldn't. Before my mother moved in, I imagined us working on our marriage, laughing and even talking about the good times with Jasmine. And now that my mother was in our home, all we did was argue and fight and I was sick of it. Yes, he was possessive sometimes but that's what happens when a man loves you.

"Denim, come here," my mother said calling out for me a bit louder.

I turned around and looked at her. She was becoming huge again. She couldn't find anybody who loved her and I put the word in the other day to kill the last man she cared about. My mother was messy but at the end of the day, she was also lonely and seeking any attention she could gain...even anger.

"Ma, you got to ease up on Bradley," I said softly while crossing my arms over my chest.

"You really don't see, do you?" she asked.

"See what?"

"He is not the same man, Denim. He is not the one you first married. He's not even the same person Grainger was in a relationship with when she had him. He's different and he's doing all he can to tear you away from me. Do you ever wonder why?"

I shook my head. "Why, mama?"

"Because he was responsible for Grainger going missing. Now I might be an old horny woman, but there's truth to my words." She paused. "He doesn't love you, he wants to possess you and there is a difference."

I couldn't take it anymore. She was driving me crazy. So I walked out of the bedroom without even responding. As I moved down the hallway and toward the living room, I saw Race talking to someone through the front door. When I walked toward her, I saw a beautiful white woman outside.

"Race, who is this?" I asked coming up behind her.

We didn't open the door for anybody we weren't expecting so I was confused. When Race turned around, I saw her glassy red eyes and knew what happened. She was drunk and not thinking straight.

"My name is Mellvue," the woman said extending her slender hand toward me. "And I'm here to speak to the Kennedy family about a very important matter. May I come in?"

CHAPTER SIX
SCARLETT

As I ogled my ten-month-old son, who I left to be raised by another family, I was in awe of his beauty. Lying on his back with a ball stuffed in his mouth and his feet in the air, he looked as if life had treated him well. That would be fine if it wasn't without me.

Maybe I thought he would be sad since his birth mother wasn't raising him or in his life. Maybe I thought he would be sad since he didn't see his father, or have a connection to how he came to be in this world. I guess that's why I didn't need to raise him.

I wasn't fit to be his mother.

"Scarlett, he's beautiful isn't he?" Nadine Walker said as she strolled out of the kitchen with a beautiful sterling silver tray with doves carved into its edges. On top of it was a pot of tea and sugar cookies. "I'm amazed every day because he has come so far. He's growing so quickly."

I gazed up at Nadine; my eyes followed her until she took a seat next to me. The scent of her expensive lavender infused fragrance hovered in the air. Whipping her long brown hair over her shoulder, the corners of her mouth rose upward in a large smile as she looked at Master.

The charm of her slender body hypnotized me. The lines of her physique were splendid as she crossed her legs and continued to gaze at Master. Although in her fifties, she didn't look a day over forty. Leaning forward, she poured me a cup of chai tea before serving herself.

"Yes, he is perfect," I said as I convinced the tears not to fall. "And he looks so peaceful, Nadine. Thank you for taking care of him."

She placed the palm of her hand on my wrist, her touch cool. "I have to ask you something I always wanted to know." She blew into the cup, causing waves to form in the tea.

"What is it?"

"Why did you leave Master on our doorstep?" she took a tiny sip and sat the cup down. "I mean when I looked at him, on the day you left him, it was evident that you cared about him. You even typed a letter indicating what his name was so that we would know."

"Thank you for honoring my request because you didn't have to."

"Nonsense. A name like Master sets him up for greatness. Of course I had to honor your request." She paused. "But why would you leave him if you wanted to remain in his life?"

Her question was warranted and I was in awe that it took her so long to ask. I re-entered his world about three months ago to the day. Surprisingly, she knew who I was the moment she saw me. Although Master was biracial, his hair was also red and at first I figured that was what gave me away.

Before responding to her question, I pondered the real answer. Originally, I gave him up because my husband told me that he was in love with another woman. I wanted to hurt him like he hurt me, knowing he desired nothing more than to be in his son's life.

I was successful in my attempt to break him. Not only did Master's kidnapping hurt him, but also he gained a lot of weight in the months since. Camp spent so much time trying to find out who kidnapped our child that he slacked in helping his brothers run the business.

I would've returned Master to him a long time ago. Even spent some time creating a story about how I found him. But since Master was gone, Camp stopped seeing his girlfriend and he stayed home with me more.

I wasn't under any illusions that he loved me like a wife again. I could tell the time he spent with me was purely out of pity. But when you love a man as much as I did Camp, you'll take what you can get. At the end of the day, if Master returned he would leave and I wasn't willing to part with him.

The other explanation of why I gave Master up might be my biggest reason. I was abused as a child and in turn, children made me nervous and jumpy. Sometimes I acted out violently. I once broke Jasmine's leg because she cried so much that I threw her in the bathtub out of anger. And when I heard Master wailing I felt myself about to do the same to him.

At the end of the day, Master was safer if he stayed with the Walkers. They were both heavy in the church and couldn't have a child of their own. In my heart, I was giving them a gift and in turn, they were giving me one by keeping him safe.

"I gave him up because my lifestyle is not conducive for a child," I said sipping the piping hot tea, burning my upper lip slightly. "And I want him to be happy and receive the love he deserves."

She picked up her cup and dropped two cubes of sugar inside. "How did you find me? Because I have a feeling giving him to me was no mistake."

I sat my cup down and pinned my arms against my belly before rubbing my elbows. "When I was pregnant I used to drive out to Virginia a lot to get away. The long drives helped me think. My marriage was in trouble at the time and the drives allowed me a temporary escape." I grabbed the teacup and took another sip before placing it down again. "On one particular day I happened on a modest-sized church. I started not to walk inside but something about your voice called out to me. You were talking about not being able to have children and I waited until the end of the service and followed you home."

Her head hung and she placed a strand of hair behind her ear. "I remember that day." She got up and walked toward the fireplace. "It was the first day my husband, or the reverend, as he likes to be called," she giggled, "found out about me being barren. Although I'm not of childbearing age anymore, he always thought it was because of him. That something was wrong with his sperm. I hated holding the secret that I learned as a teenager. And it was that my tubes were abnormal and no matter how healthy he was, as long as I was his wife, he would not be a father."

"How did he take it?"

"He handled it well in church but when we left he grew bitter and angry. We've been married for over twenty years and I wondered if our marriage would make it," she continued, shaking her head. "And then you gave us Master."

I smiled, more confident than ever that I made the right decision. Although the pastor had me thinking that there was a dark side to him.

Suddenly her lips trembled, forcing her chin to do the same. "I don't want to fall in love with him, Scarlett, if you're going to take him from us. I need to know this is real. I need to know that it's safe to love him."

I stood up and walked toward her. Grabbing both of her hands I said, "As long as you're good to my son, I'll continue to be good to you."

"It's not about the money," she said removing her hands from mine. "Although the anonymous donations you've given us have allowed us to purchase a new church." She smiled. "What I'm asking you is regarding the heart. Can I fall in love with that baby? Is it safe to do so?"

"He's yours, Nadine," I said. My words tasted like salt in my mouth although they were true. "And all I ask is that you do what you are doing now. Allow me to see him from time to time. To check on his safety."

She gripped my hands and squeezed them softly. "Then we have a deal." She leaned in and kissed me on the cheek. "But you know," she said seriously, "the reverend can never find out that you're in Master's life, or that you're donating to the church."

"Why?"

"Let's just say it wouldn't be good."

I looked into her eyes. "Nadine, are you scared of him?"

"I respect him, although sometimes it resembles fear."

When I heard my phone vibrate, I separated from her and grabbed it from my purse. It was a text message from Camp.

He decided to take our case! Come to the office now!

His face was as chalky white as death. He was an ugly man, with pus bumps all over his protruding white nose. I didn't like him for many reasons. Not only because he was unattractive but also because he was good at what he did.

His name was Morris Swanson, and he was a popular private investigator. Everybody he sought to find, he did and now he was on Camp's side.

I sat on the other side of the desk and Camp was sitting next to me, holding my hand. When I gazed over at my husband, I noticed how he looked upon Morris as if he was Jesus Christ. I never saw him look so goofy and it was obvious that he was pouring all of his hope into this man. "I really appreciate you taking our case," Camp said with a wide smile. It was as if Morris already found him in his eyes. "I know you didn't have any openings so this means a lot."

Morris shuffled a few papers around on his desk. "I am a busy man," he responded. His voice steely and uncaring.

"I know and that's why I appreciate you. I've been doing all I can to find my boy on my own and nothing has worked."

"Like I said when you first contacted me, I'll do all I can to help you," Swanson said. "But I can't make any promises."

"You have a ninety percent success rate," Camp responded. He was on his shit so hard he may as well have sucked his dick.

Arrogantly, Morris said, "Well, this is true." Morris looked over at me. "I am the best. But before I get more information, please tell me something. How did you two meet?"

What type of question is that? I thought.

"He met me when I was in court one day for a traffic ticket," I lied, shuffling a little in my seat.

Although Camp met me in a courthouse, I was deceitful on why I was there. I was being charged for abusing my daughter who Camp didn't know about. Between my secret twelve-year-old daughter who lived with my ex-husband, and Master who was staying with the Walkers, I had a lot of undisclosed information. This was the main reason I didn't need Morris snooping around in my business.

I would rather talk to the cops.

"That's interesting," he said leaning back into his chair, causing it to squeak. "So what were you there for, Mr. Kennedy?"

"Boat docking tickets I think." It was obvious Camp was not interested in speaking about when he met me.

"Oh, so you own a boat?" Swanson asked with raised fluffy grey eyebrows.

"Several," Camp responded.

I could see the jealousy spread on Morris' face and when I looked over at Camp he didn't appear to notice the man's disgust for him. Wanting to find Master blinded him to people's intentions and I didn't want to be in his office.

Besides, there was so much going on. We had beef with the Russians, Sarah was in the house walking around naked and getting on everyone's nerves, my baby was being loved on by another woman and I was stressed.

When it came to drama, I was good.

"Are you going to help us find our son?" I asked tiring of his irrelevant questions. I crossed my legs and wiggled my foot before running my hand through my red hair, stroking my scalp in the process.

He nodded. "Of course I'm going to find your son but like I told your husband before you arrived, I believe the kidnapping is an inside job."

My heart rate increased. "Why do..." I cleared my throat because my first few words sounded like I was singing an opera. "Why would you say that?" My voice was much deeper.

"I've been doing this for over twenty years, Mrs. Kennedy. And my instincts are always correct, especially since I'm told you don't want to get the cops involved. If I'm being honest about my background, I must also be honest about what I'm about to say next. I told your husband that I don't trust you."

I felt dizzy. It was like the room was spinning and I looked at Camp and he squeezed my hand compassionately.

"Of course, he told me you weren't involved," he continued. "And that I needed to look for a man by the name of..." he searched through a few papers on his desk before stopping at one, "Ngozi, an ex-boyfriend of yours who claims to have him. But I can't seem to find any information on him."

Trying to appear offended as opposed to guilty, I said, "So you're saying I hurt my own child?"

"I don't know what you would do to him but I do know this." He sat back in his squeaky chair. "If nothing else, Mrs. Kennedy, I will find out."

We were riding in the car in silence. Every so often, Camp would clutch the steering wheel, causing his brown knuckles to whiten with each grip. Finally, he looked over at me and said, "I know I've asked you this a million times so forgive me if I'm repeating myself. But when was the last time you saw Master?"

I leaned back and looked up at the ceiling. Ten minutes out of Morris' office and already he doubted me. "Camp, why are you doing this? I've told you everything I know. I'm just as confused as you are about where our son is. We are a team; don't let him break us up."

"Humor me," he said firmly. "Tell me what happened again."

I cleared my throat and said, "You and I broke up and I got with Ngozi for a little while. It was when you were missing." I wiped my sweaty hands on my jeans. "But I didn't want to be with him because I wanted to work on our marriage. He got upset about it and told me to meet him somewhere so we could talk. I foolishly went and he kidnapped Master, Camp. That's what happened."

He looked at me and then back at the road.

"Do you believe me?" I asked.

Silence.

"Camp, do you believe me?"

CHAPTER SEVEN
BAMBI

What was Race thinking? I had to blink my eyes several times because I couldn't believe that she allowed a stranger into our home. Yet there I was, sitting on my recliner across from a woman who claimed to be a police officer. She had credentials and even a marked car out front of the house but something didn't feel right. Years in the military taught me to respect my instincts and they were going off majorly.

As I stared at this bitch, Race stood next to the door and Denim sat on the same couch as the unwanted visitor.

I could tell she had a recently blackened eye, no matter how much makeup she painted on.

"So have the police found a suspect in the burglaries?" I asked looking her up and down. Examining each of her features so that I could remember details later. "Or is he still at large?"

She turned her head towards me, allowing her hair to fall down the front of her right shoulder. "We have a few people in mind but we aren't certain they will lead to an actual suspect. These things could take days or even weeks to solve." She looked around the living room and at the tops of the walls.

Maybe for cameras.

They were all over the place but out of view.

"Can I offer you any more water?" Race asked.

The woman who introduced herself as Mellvue Harper raised her frosted glass and said, "No. I still have some." She took a large sip. "But thank you anyway."

"If you don't have any suspects why are you here?" I questioned.

"Mainly because I wanted to alert the other people in the neighborhood. These are very dark days and one must always be careful."

"I agree," I smiled. "You never know who or what you're dealing with. Some people are more deadly than others." I stared deeply into her eyes so that she knew that the threat was real.

She crossed her legs and looked at me slyly. "I concur." She paused. "The sad part is that most deaths can be prevented."

"Oh?" I responded sarcastically. "Please explain."

"Well since most murders are committed by a killer who knows his victim well, one would have to ask himself what could've been done to prevent it."

"And your theory is?" Denim asked.

"Well for starters, bringing in a mediator can always lead to a resolution but ridding relationships of greed can also do wonders. Because if both parties were willing to share and be fair, the world would not be full of envy."

"Some things are not meant to be shared," I explained, referring to Mitch. "And some parties are going to have to understand that."

She looked into my eyes and the smile vanished from her face. She blinked a few times and said, "Who really knows why people kill. Or rob for that matter." She shrugged. "I'm simply telling everyone in the area to be cautious because something dark is coming." She looked at Race. "And you must be careful in the future, darling. Because you really can't let just anybody into your home these days." She looked down at her designer jeans and white top. "I'm dressed plainly and all I had to do was flash you a badge and I was able to enter. If I were the enemy, I could've attacked."

I looked over at Race who looked away from me. The unwanted visitor was right and we all knew it.

"Well we appreciate you letting us know," Denim said. "And we'll make sure our family is aware too. So that we can be ready to defend ourselves if need be."

She stood up and shook all of our hands. I observed her professional manicure and then her makeup and hair. There wasn't a thing about this bitch out of place. She belonged to a rich man and I had a feeling that one of the Russians turned her loose.

"It was nice meeting you, Ms. Arkadi," I said with a grin. I took a guess on which brother she belonged to. And by the look on her face, I figured I guessed right.

Her eyes widened and she looked as if she saw a ghost. "What did you call me?"

"Mellvue," I responded. "What did you think I called you?"

She flapped her eyes a few times and cleared her throat. "You ladies have a good night," she said before walking out. "I'll be in contact."

I strutted over to the window by the door, pushed the cream curtain to the side and watched her get into her car. "I guess you know by now she's with the Russians," I said still staring out the window. When she was out of view I turned around and faced them. "What were you thinking, Race? What if she would've killed one of us?"

She walked over to the sofa and flopped down. "She said she was a cop, Bambi. And since we deal drugs, I figured we'd let her in to prevent any trouble."

"Race, get your head out of your fucking ass! We don't have to let nobody in here, cop or not, without a warrant! What is going on with you lately?"

"Nothing, Bambi," she pleaded. "And I didn't know she was with the Russians until you called her Arkadi's name," she said leaning against the wall. "I'm sorry."

"Did you find the specialized killer I asked for?" I asked. "Because his first job will be killing that bitch."

"With all of the men we have, I can't think of a single one who I would trust with this responsibility. But I promise on everything I love, the Kennedy name too, that I will find someone. I will not let you down." She paused. "Again."

"Race, if you can't do what needs to be done, then perhaps you don't need to have a firm position in the business."

"Bambi—"

"Bambi, shit," I yelled. "Get it together, Race. Now! This family needs you!"

I saw a tear hang in the corner of her eye but she wiped it away.

"Why would the Russians send her in here?" Denim asked returning to the subject. "If they knew where we lived, they'd just blow the bitch up. Not send in some trophy wife."

"They fucking with us," I explained. "They engaging us in a game of mental warfare before they attack. Besides, they want Mitch and until they know his whereabouts, they can't get rid of us." I paused. "We're going to have to move to the bunker tonight. Even with the soldiers we have surrounding the perimeter of our house, it's best to be safe than sorry."

"I don't feel like moving again," Denim sighed as she pulled a blunt from her jean pocket and lit it.

By T. Styles

"Between my mother and Bradley, I've been stressed out lately. Moving right now is not on my agenda."

I sat next to her. Ever since Bradley came home, we hadn't had a chance to talk about how she felt. I wasn't sure how she was handling having him back and dealing with not having Jasmine. Denim was tough but I could tell things were weighing on her and her mother wasn't helping matters in the least.

"Can I do anything for you?" I asked honestly. "We haven't had a chance to talk because every time I try to get with you, Bradley grabs you." I paused. "Even though I understand the need for him to be around his wife, I miss us."

She sighed. "Just you guys being here means a lot to me." She looked over at Race.

"Is there anything else I can do to make things easier?" I persisted.

"If you can get my mother to wear some clothes around here, that would be a start."

Race shook her head. "She walked in on me and Ramirez in our bedroom with that outfit on too," Race said.

"Girl, your mother is a fucking mess," I laughed. "The other day I came home and found her in my bed. I think she was waiting on Kevin and was mad when she got me instead. I read her a new ass before I kicked her out my room."

"I'm so sorry, ya'll," she said between soft giggles. "If I knew where Grainger was she wouldn't be here but she's a wreck without having her around. Someone has to always be watching my mother."

I bit down on my bottom lip and looked over at Race. She looked away. The guilt of knowing that Race and I killed Grainger bothered me daily, especially when I stared into Denim's eyes. Denim and I may not have been blood related but I loved her like we were sisters and I hated keeping secrets from family.

Denim needed Bradley but if I told her that he gave the word to have her sister killed so she couldn't testify against him in court, she would've been devastated. They fed off of each other and Denim had to be with him, especially with Jasmine gone.

After so much time, I thought Denim would be smart enough to know that Grainger was dead but she seemed to be holding onto hope that she was strung out and doped up somewhere. She may have realized the truth if Sarah wasn't around.

I still remember the day Race and I murdered her.

Earlier in the week, we met with Bradley in the jail because he was locked up for raping Grainger. Although he denied doing it, I believed he did the moment I saw his eyes. But it wasn't about judgment, Bradley was family and that was the bottom line.

In the meeting, he had one request for us...to kill Grainger.

Since Grainger was always more trouble than she was worth, Race and me put her out of her misery. And chopped her up in so many pieces she'd never be found whole.

"Listen, no matter where Grainger is, you deserve to be happy, Denim," I said softly to her. "You do know that don't you?"

She held her head down and a tear rolled down her cheek. She placed her hand over mine and looked into my eyes. "Not knowing where she is, that's harder than anything. I really have to find her, Bambi. I have to!"

After my conversation with Denim, I got on the phone and called the east coast bosses. My family and me had to move again and I needed to know that the bosses had our back if it was time for war. We couldn't fight the Russians alone. We needed manpower.

The only thing was, not all of them reported to me. Although a few got their cocaine directly from us, most received their work from Mitch. So I couldn't make them do anything they didn't want.

Still, I wanted to alert them that the Russians were moving in on the east coast and that if they were successful in killing us and getting Mitch, their cocaine supply would be cut short.

One by one, I made the calls and my disappointment grew with each contact made. Although some were nice, they each shared the same position...that the beef with the Russians was a Kennedy Kings issue, not an east coast one.

Frustrated, I walked out of my study, grabbed a glass from the cabinet and the vodka bottle from the freezer. Since I gave up sobriety, there were good days and bad days in my life. Sometimes I handled my liquor well and others I didn't.

I had drunk days that were so bad that I would get up and everybody in the house would be mad at me. Half of the time, I didn't know what I did wrong and after awhile they were used to it. As much as I wished I never picked up the bottle when Kevin disappeared, I knew there was no going back now. I was going to drink and my family would have to accept it.

After pouring three glasses and downing them all, I was buzzed. I figured I needed to call my husband to give him and update on Mellvue being in our home.

Sitting on the couch, I crossed my legs and dialed his number. After three rings, the phone picked up. "Kevin, you have a minute?" I sighed. "Something happened."

Silence.

I heard someone moving in the background but I didn't hear him respond. "Kevin, are you there?" I frowned.

When I pressed the phone closer to my ear I realized his cell was probably in his pocket and he answered by mistake. I told him over and over that shit like that was going to get him in trouble. I guess he didn't give a fuck.

I was about to hit the end button but instead, I listened. Since we didn't talk anymore, I was curious to find out what kinds of things he did when we weren't together.

I got my answer.

I felt gut punched when I heard his voice followed by that of a woman. "Kevin, stop playing," the girl giggled. "You always talking shit but you never back it up. I'ma stop fucking with your sexy ass."

"I'm serious," he responded. "You...me wanting to pull this car over. Why you wear...dress?" I couldn't make out a few of his words but I got the gist of the conversation. He was with a chick that he must've been so attracted to that he wanted to fuck her on sight.

I was trembling.

My heart hurt.

Kevin was mine whether I wanted him or not.

She giggled again and I was hoping he would say her name so that I could locate this bitch and have her murdered by night's end. Because although Kevin and me weren't together, I was still his wife and every bitch on the east coast knew it.

"Don't talk about it, be about it," she responded. "You already know I'm ready when you are. So let me see that chocolate dick."

The phone must've been moving around because I heard some muffled voices and then suddenly things were clearer. He said, "Shhhhh." I guess he took the phone out of his pocket and realized it was on. "Hello," he finally said. "Bambi?"

Humiliated enough already, I hung up.

I tossed the phone on the couch, leaned back and looked up at the ceiling. What kind of life was this? Why was I even still in this marriage? I was rich and scared for my life. A mother and yet I felt childless. And I was married to a man who was making it clear that he didn't want me.

I knew Kevin and I had problems but dealing with another woman while he still slept in my bed messed up my head. I know I was wrong for fucking his cousin but I didn't have a choice. The nigga was blackmailing me. And I fucked him for family and to stay out of jail.

Playing her voice over and over in my mind, I was surprised how badly my feelings hurt. I wasn't supposed to show emotion. I was Bambi Kennedy, of the Pretty Kings, and I was strong.

If all that was true, why did it hurt so much?

When my phone rang, without looking I knew who it was. My cheating ass husband. But in that moment I made a decision not to answer. If he wanted to carry shit like it was really over then all I could say was, let the games begin.

MELLVUE

After returning the marked police car to the warehouse, Mellvue took a shower at the Ritz-Carlton Hotel and slid into her Versace dress and three thousand dollar heels. Back to her old self, she slipped into her silver Aston Martin and called Arkadi, her fiancé.

The sound of the phone ringing through the Bluetooth speakers filled the car as she glided into traffic. Speaking in her native Russian tongue, she updated him on the status of her mission. "I told you they would let me inside," she said smiling brightly. "If only you let me help you more, your troubles would be over."

"Lyubov Moya Mellvue, I didn't doubt you once," he chuckled.

She grinned and looked at her face in the rearview mirror. Using her pinky finger, she cleaned up the red lipstick that smeared toward the corners of her mouth. "But you said they were smart. That they may not believe I was a police officer and to respect the chorn. But you were wrong. They allowed me into their home and they believed everything I said. If you ask me, they aren't so smart."

Angry that Mellvue didn't respect the Kennedys as viable threats, he snapped. "It would be as great a mistake not to take them as reputable threats as it would be to not take me as one."

Remembering the times he beat her for insubordination, she clutched the steering wheel tighter and swallowed. "I didn't mean to say things in that way."

"And yet you spoke disrespectfully anyway," he responded. *"Should I remind you how to speak to me and then purchase you another set of teeth again?"*

"No, dear," she said in a low voice.

"Then let me be clear. You don't get to the level they're on in this business without having wits. And the moment you forget that when you come in contact with a Kennedy, you will die."

Mellvue whipped her brown hair over her shoulders. She didn't respect black people and she certainly didn't think they were smarter than her. *"I understand,"* she said softly. *"I merely wanted you to know that you have them right where you want them. All you have to do is make a move and end this war."*

"And when I deem that time to be right I will do just that. Now, who else was in the Bunke?"

"One woman with blue dreadlocks, another with a brown bob and some woman with long hair, fatigue pants and a scar on her face."

"This woman with scar...was she also beautiful?"

"Yes, as far as niggers are concerned." *She paused.* *"Why?"*

He laughed softly. *"That was my sweet Bambi. You may not know this but I put that scar on her beautiful face myself. I wanted every day she woke up and looked in the mirror to be a reminder of me and Iakov."*

Mellvue caught his amusement and grew jealous. *"No, honey, I wasn't aware."* *She gritted her teeth in an attempt to hide her jealousy.*

"It's amazing that with all the money she possesses she still hasn't had the scar removed. I think she's wearing it as badge of honor. She's proud of scar as I was to give it to her. That's mark of true soldier."

Mellvue rolled her eyes. *"So what are you going to do now, Arkadi? Attack?"*

"We'll make a move later. If Bambi was there, she's smart enough to know who you are and that we are coming for Mitch, wherever he may be. I'm sure she's packing the family up and moving them as we speak."

"So why did you send me there?"

"I have my reasons. One of them is because I wanted her to know that she's touchable. And that soon, very soon, their empire will crumble."

CHAPTER EIGHT
KEVIN
TWO WEEKS LATER

*W*omen twirled around the poles like snakes within the dark Smack Back strip club. The Kennedy Kings lay back comfortably on a red velvet semi-circle couch with stacks of one hundred dollar bills piled in front of them on the table. With all the beauty to behold, Kevin had one thing on his mind, his wife.

While it was true that the Kennedys were at war outside the house, he was also at war inside himself. He had a feeling that he accidently answered the phone when Bambi called some weeks back and she overheard him but she never mentioned it. Instead, she started sleeping in one of the extra rooms in the new bunker they moved into. And instead of being angry, she treated him extra nice, even making him breakfast a few times although he refused to eat it for fear it would be poisoned.

He hated her coolness and yet there was no other woman he wanted to be with in the world, including the nurse he was squiring about town on the day Bambi called.

When a group of women who hadn't touched the dance floor wiggled toward their section, each brother made way for them. Not being able to wait, Bradley snatched up a light-skinned girl with a big booty and yelled, "Let me see that ass wiggle."

Kevin and the other brothers felt that ever since Bradley returned from jail, he was trying harder to appear tough. He didn't know what was going on with him but he hoped that soon he would return to his normal self.

As the night went on, Kevin poured each of his brothers a glass of champagne. He raised his in the air. "We don't get to do this shit a lot so I'm gonna make a toast," Kevin said. "To blood, to money, to us." Kevin looked over at Camp. He had his glass in the air but the solemn look of missing his son never left his face. It was a permanent part of his features. His kidnapping was always on his mind. "And to my little nephew who we will find, no matter what we gotta do and who we gotta do it to," Kevin continued.

Each man raised his glass and took a sip. Although the beauty on his lap was doing her thing, Kevin was interested in the tall chick with green eyes on the dance floor.

"Who's that, mama?" he asked the stripper.

She turned her slender neck, looked at the stage and rolled her eyes. "That's Romance. Why?"

"Do me a favor." He peeled a band off one of the stacks and handed her a one hundred dollar bill. "How 'bout you get up and tell old girl I want to see her."

She stuffed the money in her bra and rolled her eyes. "Whatever," she responded stomping away.

"That was cold as shit," Ramirez laughed. "You in this joint hurting strippers' feelings for no reason." He paused. "She was thick. Why you send her on her way?"

"Not everybody be in this joint wifing bitches like you and Race," Kevin responded.

"Damn," Bradley laughed. "You sliced that nigga's heart," he continued as the dark-skinned cutie hovered her tight ass over top of his crotch.

"I just go after what I want," Kevin replied.

By T. Styles

"So why you not going after your wife?" Camp responded as he sipped a beer and whispered something in the stripper's ear that caused her to get up and stomp out of VIP.

"Before I answer that question, what you tell shawty?" Kevin asked looking at the stripper.

"I told her to get the fuck off my lap. She kept leaning on my shirt and shit." He dusted something off of Master's face. "Now answer the question. Why you not back with Bambi?"

"Because she don't know how to respect a man," he responded. "I think Bambi believes she a dude sometimes." His brothers didn't know that Bambi was responsible for their aunt's death or that she fucked Cloud before he was killed and he decided to keep it that way. That alone was the main reason for their beef.

"Ain't that one of the things you liked about her?"

Kevin looked across the club at the tall cutie who was getting off the pole and coming his way. "I'm done with Bambi. Sometimes you marry a person and when you see who they really are you realize you made a mistake."

His brothers laughed, not one of them believing it was over.

"That's how I feel about Scarlett," Camp said. "I know she wants to be with me but I'm done with her."

"This shit is wild," Ramirez said. "Kevin and Bambi don't want each other. Camp doesn't want Scarlett. Bradley is obsessed with his wife and Race doesn't want shit to do with me even though she lets me eat her pussy every other night." He laughed. "What the fuck is going on with the Kennedy family?"

The brothers laughed heartedly.

Roman walked up to Kevin. The first thing that grabbed him was her sparkling green eyes. "May I sit down?"

Kevin smiled and looked over at Ramirez. "Ain't nothing going on with the Kennedy family. We good. Besides, as long as I got my brothers, the rest of this shit is trivial." He took Romance's hand. "Of course you can sit down, beautiful. That's why I called you over."

By T. Styles

CHAPTER NINE
DENIM

The cool toilet seat was uncomfortable as I peed on a stick inside of the luxury bunker that Bambi had built for us. Bradley was standing beside me rubbing my back as if I was already about to give birth. I could feel his excitement and it made me tense.

I loved this man so much that sometimes it hurt. And I also knew that things were about to get crazy with the Russians taking direct fire at us. I even had visions about burying someone under a Kennedy cloth. And since I was having the dream personally, I figured it was my husband. With all that said, the last thing I needed was another baby. But as sick as I'd been lately, I might not have had a choice.

When I pulled the stick out from between my legs Bradley took it out of my hands and sat it on the sink. Instead of getting up right away, I remained sitting on the toilet. "How were the dancers tonight?" I asked, still smelling the liquor on his body.

"How you know we went to the strip club?"

"You smell like cheap Victoria's Secret body spray."

He laughed. "It was aight." He looked at the stick again and then back at me. "You said you didn't mind so I figured it was cool." He shrugged.

"Bradley, I don't mind you going out, especially with your brothers. Besides, none of them bitches got shit on me and I'm not that shallow. I just wish you gave me the same freedom." I paused. "I mean, why don't you like me hanging out with Bambi and them?"

"It's not that I don't like you hanging out. We all live together. Ya'll kick it here all the time."

"You know what I mean."

"It's like this. Bambi, Scarlett and Race's marriages are fucked up. And I don't want their shit rubbing off on you. If that's wrong, then kill me."

"But they never do that," I said seriously. "Not once have they said anything negative about our marriage."

"Not even Bambi?" he asked with one raised brow.

"Not one of them, Bradley. I wouldn't stand for it."

He shook his head and looked at the stick again. "Damn, how long does this shit take?"

I glanced at it and then back at him. "If I am...you know...pregnant...what do you want to do about it?"

His forehead crinkled and his teeth clenched. "Why would you even ask me some shit like that?" His voice was heavy. "You my wife and anything we make together is perfect." He paused. "That's what the fuck I'm talking 'bout! Who would put some shit like that in your head? That aborting our baby is even an option?"

I hunched over and rested my elbows on my thighs. Clasping my hands together, I looked up at my husband again. "Bradley, we are at war." I reached out for his hand and he stuffed it into his pocket. I guess he didn't want to touch me. Dropping my hand to my side, I asked, "You do understand that, right?"

"Yeah, but what that got to do with me and you having another child?"

"It has a lot to do with you. Kevin and Ramirez need your help with the operation. With the Russians hanging around, my sisters and me need your help too. Not only that, neither of us have time to be parents. It's just not safe."

"Camp is around. He got their backs."

"Be real, Bradley! Camp is so caught up in trying to find Master that he's not available to your brothers. And although I understand that, it doesn't take away from the fact that we need a plan and we need all hands on deck." I sighed. "Having a baby right now is not a good idea. Can't you see that?"

Bradley exhaled and wiped his hands over his face. He looked up at the ceiling and then back at me. "If you are pregnant now it means it's the right time." He turned around and looked at the pee stick.

My stare remained on him and I knew the answer before he even told me because his cheeks rose and stiffened.

"You pregnant, bay." He showed me the stick.

He waved it in the air like a faggy and I was so mad!

"God is giving us another chance to get it right," he yelled.

I slapped the tissue, grabbed a few squares and wiped my pussy. Irritated, I slammed the tissue in the bowl and flushed the toilet. I didn't even bother to wash my hands.

Now everything I'd been feeling made sense. The morning sickness, the body aches and even my anger. I was a mother all over again before I even got the chance to mourn the loss of my last child.

I flopped on the edge of the bed and I could feel him right behind me. I needed breathing room but he was always in my space. "I'm scared, Bradley." I put my hand over my chest. "I feel it in my heart that this is the wrong time. I've been having dreams about murder in this family. Every night I watch a casket being dropped into the ground with a black sheet over it. Do you want to know what the word on the cloth says?"

He shrugged as if he couldn't care less.

"It says Kennedy." I paused. "Aren't you worried?"

He sat next to me, turned my chin toward him and looked in my eyes. "First off, I'm not going nowhere and neither is anybody in this family. Look at where we live," he chuckled. "The President of the United States of America ain't as secure as we are in here. We have armed men surrounding the property and at every entrance of our home. We good and you need to feel safe."

"That's just it. I don't!" I yelled.

He took a deep breath. "When you talk like this it makes me feel like you think I can't protect you. It makes me feel like you don't trust me."

"That's not it, Bradley."

"I'm your husband, Denim! You ain't single and you won't be if you have our baby. I will never leave your side. Ever! Not even in death!" he screamed. "You gotta remember that, baby. Or else you gonna be in the same shoes as Scarlett, Bambi and Race."

My body felt like it crumpled over. "What are you trying to say?" I whispered.

"You know what I'm saying," he said standing up. "We the only couple in this house right now still in love. Don't give that up because you want to abort my baby. If you do, I will never forgive you. And it's important that you understand that shit."

He stomped toward the door and I didn't notice that my mother was standing there. Watching. He walked around her and frowned and she eased inside. She sat next to me and said, "So you're pregnant?"

I shook my head preparing to say no but I cried out instead. In that moment, my mother did something she hadn't in a long time. She gripped me closer and rubbed my shoulders. Just having the touch from my mother made me more vulnerable and weak. I rubbed my palm against my chest trying to relieve some of the pressure on my heart.

"Come here, baby," she said pulling me. "Sit on my lap."

I got up and sat on her legs. Although I felt like an idiot, she rocked me in her arms like she did when I was a child.

"It's okay, baby," she said softly. "No matter what happens, everything will work out."

Something happened in that instant. At that moment, I wasn't Denim the drug boss anymore, I was a child and she was my mother.

After crying my eyes out, I looked up at her and said, "Mama, I don't know what I'm going to do. If I have this baby, I think something terrible will happen. I keep seeing death."

"Then don't have it."

"But I don't want to lose Bradley either. I can't put him through another loss."

"Why did you tell him that you might be?"

"I thought he was going to be out later than he was. The plan was to take the pregnancy test alone but he showed up." I paused. "I really don't want to have this baby. It doesn't feel right."

"Then don't," she responded. "It's your body."

"But he's my husband."

She wiped the tears off my face with her dry palm. "Honey, Bradley is trying to replace Jasmine," she said in a soft voice. "Don't let him do that to you or himself. If you feel now is not the time, then he has to respect that."

"Mama, he isn't trying to replace Jasmine," I said as I stood up and then plopped on the bed in a ball on my side. "He just wants another baby, that's all. He misses Jasmine as much as I do."

"He is trying to replace her, Denim. You can't have this baby." She paused. "Don't you remember what you went through being a mother to an autistic child? You were miserable and you didn't have a life."

I popped up and moved across the room, away from her. "I loved my fucking baby! And it never mattered to me that she was autistic!"

"I'm not saying you didn't love her but I do know this, you were overwhelmed. Bradley wasn't with Jasmine as much as you were. He left you to care for everything on your own and if you have this child now, it will be just like Jasmine. Autistic." She paused. "So why do that to yourself? You haven't even found out why you had an autistic child to begin with. How do you know you won't have another?" She touched my leg. "Don't let that man tell you when to have a baby, Denim. It will be a major mistake. For everyone."

CHAPTER TEN
RACE

My sisters and me were in the Relaxation Room inside of the cozy bunker. I had to admit, although I didn't want to move again, Bambi went out of her way to make sure that the new hideout was nothing short of luxurious. Every room had a California King sized bed, flat wall TV and fur carpets. Every bedroom had a private bathroom with gold accents and heated floors.

This place was fit for kings.

It was fit for Kennedys.

The Relaxation Room was fucking heaven. There were twelve large money green velvet recliners and thick brown curtains on the floor-to-ceiling windows.

In this place it felt like we weren't in seclusion and that was part of its beauty and terror. Inside there, you could almost forget that trouble was coming.

That we were at war.

We were sitting in the Jacuzzi trying to unwind. We hadn't had a chance to really talk to each other and I missed our conversations.

A little buzzed, Bambi tied her hair into a high bun to prevent it from getting wet. She grabbed her glass off the edge of the tub and looked at me. "Have you found a killer for me yet, Race?"

I sighed. Lately my mind had been all over the place and I knew Bambi was starting to believe that I couldn't handle things. That couldn't be further from the truth but it was getting harder to prove her wrong. "Not yet," I responded. "But I'm—"

"Working on it," she said finishing my sentence.

"I just need a little more time, Bambi. That's it." I paused. "I promise I won't let you down."

"I have to tell you all something," Denim said as she sat a little higher in the Jacuzzi. I was so happy she took the heat off me I smiled at her.

"What's up?" I asked.

She looked down and then at all of us again. "I'm pregnant."

"Congratulations," we all said happily as we moved in for a hug. Bambi was so excited that she accidently knocked the bun out of Denim's dreadlocks when she gripped her up. As we clutched each other, with our breasts mushed together in an embrace, I noticed that Denim was not hugging us back.

Slowly I moved away from her and Scarlett and Bambi followed my lead.

"As you can see, I'm not happy about this shit," she said under her breath. "It's not the right time." She rubbed her belly.

"Fuck is you talking about?" Bambi yelled. "If you pregnant it's the right time."

"You sound like Bradley."

"She's right," I said. "It would be different if you weren't happily married, Denim. That man loves you and I know he would love the baby. If anything, you being pregnant is a good thing, not the other way around."

"Why would it be different if she wasn't happily married?" Scarlett asked. She was the only one out of all of us who got her hair wet. It was smoothed back and tied in a ponytail, which draped down her back and stuck to her damp pale skin. "If she isn't ready for a baby, she isn't ready for a baby. Happily married or not."

"Since when have you taken up for Denim?" I questioned suspiciously.

"We have our problems but I understand what it means to not be ready for a child."

"Well if you not ready for a child maybe you shouldn't fuck," I responded.

"Let's talk about something else," Bambi said, obviously trying to skip the subject.

I wondered why.

"No, let's not talk about something else," Scarlett said abruptly. She looked at me, Denim and then Bambi. "I have to tell them. I'm sorry, Bambi."

Bambi's eyes widened and she shook her head. "Please don't do it, Scarlett. Now is not a good time. Just let it go."

"Don't do what?" I asked. "Are ya'll holding secrets again? Because I'm sick of that shit."

"Me too," Denim responded. "Seems like whenever something is going on in this family, you two know way before the rest of us."

"That's because all you want to do is smoke weed," Bambi said to Denim. Bambi looked at me. "And all you want to do is have threesomes with Ramirez. Whenever I need someone to talk to, Scarlett is always here. She's always available."

"That's a low blow," I responded. "Me and Ram haven't fucked a bitch since I killed Carey, so I don't even know what you talking about." The moment I revealed my secret about Carey's death, I knew I made a mistake. I didn't tell my friends what happened to our side chick although Bambi had her ideas.

I didn't tell anybody because I didn't want to talk about it. Plus every time I remembered that day, it brought up pain.

It was over a year ago and Ramirez and I made a decision that she was not good for our marriage and I thought it was done. But when I came home early one day she was in my room, with him.

Alone.

Jealous, angry and hurt I killed her and buried her body on our other property. What hurt me was not that she was there but that Ramirez loved her as much as me and I had a problem with that.

After admitting to Carey's death, I sat back in the Jacuzzi and I could feel their eyes all over me. I guess they all wanted to know what happened to Carey.

"I thought you said she left on her own," Denim said with a hung jaw.

"She had a little assistance," I said under my breath. Trying to get the subject back off me, I decided to put it back where it belonged. Besides, it wasn't the first time I committed murder and it wouldn't be the last. "So what did you want to tell us, Scarlett?"

Everyone remained silent for a while before we focused on her.

Everyone but Bambi. She was still looking directly at me.

"I know where Master is," Scarlett said softly. "I've always known."

We all moved in closer. "What the fuck you mean you know where he is?"

"I know where he is," she repeated. "And he's safe."

Denim's face got a shade redder. Her eyebrows lowered and pinched together. "Why isn't my nephew here, Scarlett?" she yelled. "If you know where he is, why isn't he here? It doesn't make any sense!"

"He's with a better family," she whispered.

"Fuck is that supposed to mean?" I yelled. "What's better than a Kennedy except another Kennedy?"

"You tell me, Race?" Scarlett asked. "Seeing as how you're trying to get a divorce and all."

Low blow.

"Where is he?" Denim yelled snatching the mike.

"He's with a Christian family because my current lifestyle is too much for a baby right now. I mean, look at us. We're drug dealers who have Russians chasing us. I can't—"

"Bitch, the fact that we have Russians trying to kill us is an even bigger reason why he should be with us," Denim yelled. "How do we know they won't try to kill him for revenge? There's no fucking excuse for him not to be home!" She paused. "With his family! Where he belongs! Do you know what I would give to have Jasmine back? Do you?"

"Calm down, Denim," Bambi said. "It's more to the story than Scarlett is letting on."

"Don't fucking tell me to calm down!" she screamed at her. "How could you hear that man cry out every night for his son when you know where he is?" Denim asked turning her attention back to Scarlett. "How could you watch him fall to his knees and hold his chest whenever he thinks about his baby?" she continued as she got up and approached Scarlett. "You don't know how many nights I got on my knees and prayed that Master was okay when I heard that man cry! And the whole time you know where he was. You're a fucking monster! You should do the world a favor and kill yourself."

Bambi stood up and separated her from Scarlett. "Instead of getting mad, you need to thank God that your prayers were answered, Denim," Bambi said.

"Because if it's true that you prayed that Master was okay, then you got your wish."

Denim looked at Bambi, rolled her eyes and sat down. The Jacuzzi bubbles surrounded her.

"Don't worry, shit is about to crash down around me," Scarlett said.

"What you mean?" I asked.

"Camp hired a private detective who is out to get me," Scarlett continued. "Since I told Camp that Ngozi said we shouldn't get the police involved, now he's going this route. Seeking private help." She sighed. "From the best."

"You know when he finds out he'll never forgive you right?" Denim said softly. "You said you loved him, Scarlett. And I hope you're prepared for the aftermath because it won't turn out good. Bring his son back. Bring my nephew home."

Scarlett's head dropped and her white skin splotched up right before our eyes. "I know he won't forgive me but now is not the time."

"Can you live with that?" Denim continued.

"Right now, I don't have a choice."

"Listen, only Scarlett knows why she gave her baby up," Bambi said. "And we have to honor that."

"Fuck that, I need to know where my nephew lives," I said. I was going to respect her need for privacy but if I found out my nephew was being harmed in any way then there was going to be problems.

Christian family or not.

"I want the information too," Denim said.

"I'll give it to all of you," Scarlett said softly. "But you can't visit when the reverend is at home."

"So how is he?" I asked Scarlett.

Scarlett smiled but then it drifted away. "He's beautiful. Hair as red as mine and eyes as big as Texas." Her face was wet with water and sweat but I could still see she was crying. "Never knew a baby could grow up so well without his mother. I guess I do now."

Denim hopped up and walked over to Scarlett. She stared at her for a second before raising her hand and smacking her in the face. "That's for Camp." Before Bambi could reach her, Denim smacked her again. "That's for me."

Bambi was about to jack Denim up but she hopped out of the Jacuzzi, snatched her towel off the chair and stormed out of the Relaxation Room.

Her ass jiggling with each stomp.

Bambi was about to go after her but Scarlett said, "Let her go, Bambi. Please."

Bambi sat down and shook her head. "You shouldn't have told her unless you wanted Master back, Scarlett. That was a bad move. You know how that girl is."

Scarlett's face was red with Denim's handprint.

"Who says I don't want him back?" she said softly.

Bambi exhaled. "So when are we going to get him then?"

"Not now, but soon."

"Well, whenever it's time you know we're on top of it," Bambi responded before raising her glass and sipping her drink.

"What's going on with you and Kevin, Bambi?" I asked.

"Besides the fact that we have rough sex and don't talk?"

"Yeah."

"I think he's seeing somebody else," she said. "But what can I do?"

"Fight for him," Scarlett said softly. "If I thought Camp wanted me back I would." She looked out into the room. "I would do anything for the slightest ounce of attention from him."

Considering what she did to Master, I believed her and that made her more dangerous than all of us.

"I think it's over for real now," Bambi continued. "He gonna do him and I'm gonna do me. I guess I have to leave it like that."

"You sure about that?"

"Right now we are at war with the Russians, Race. The only thing on my mind is bringing resolution to this shit. I'll worry about Kevin and his bum bitches later."

CHAPTER ELEVEN
BAMBI

Kevin stood before the cherry wood table in the dining room of the Bunker to discuss the status of our business. Just like other family meetings, at this one everybody was present.

"As you know, business has been down for the last three weeks," Kevin said.

"Not to mention the fact that Larry has murdered more of our men and their family members than we can spare," Race said. "This nigga has no heart."

"To top it all off, some of our most loyal soldiers have jumped ship and moved on with other dealers."

"If they jumped ship they weren't loyal," Ramirez said. "What I care about a fuck nigga if he has no respect for the brand?" He sank deeper into his chair with a glass of fine cognac in his hand.

He was snappy and I knew it was because of the conversation Race and him had earlier. I heard her screaming about wanting a divorce and that once there was resolution with the Russians she would be moving out.

With or without his signature.

"It doesn't mean that they aren't loyal," Race said with her words slurring a little. I knew she was drunk and if I noticed that, it was major. If I looked one ounce of what she looked like while handling business, I had a new resolve to quit.

"At the end of the day they have families to take care of and if no money's on the streets they still got to eat," Race continued. "That's why we have to get at the Reapers and the Russians, and end this shit once and for all."

"She's right," Bradley said as he rubbed Denim's shoulders as she sat on his lap. When I looked at Denim's face she seemed annoyed by his touch and I knew why. "If we don't make a move now we're not going to have any men left. But we have to weigh the costs. Wars are expensive."

"Yeah, what are we going to do?" Camp asked, his eyes heavy with bags from depression.

"We have to lay low until—"

"We can't lay low," I said cutting Kevin off. "We have to move now." I pointed a stiff finger into the table.

Everyone looked at me and Kevin frowned before folding his arms over his chest. Since the fellas came back, I had no problems letting them run the business just as long as they moved the operation forward and not sideways.

"And how do we do that?" Kevin questioned me.

"We attack," I said simply.

He laughed. "Bambi, you haven't been in this business for long so let me school you right quick. These are Russians. They aren't Bay-Bay and Mo Quick from east Baltimore. You don't move on people of this caliber like it ain't nothing. You must have a plan or don't speak."

"She might not have been in business long but under her leadership, we held shit down in your absence," Scarlett said looking at the men. "So for sure she deserves the right to speak here."

"Get off Bambi's dick," Ramirez said.

"Easy, brother," Camp responded.

I winked at Scarlett and crossed my legs.

"To Scarlett's point, we made a profit too," Race added.

"Fifty percent higher at that," Denim continued.

Kevin smacked is teeth. "Even if all that was true, under your administration there wasn't an enemy who was directly attacking the brand," Kevin said. "When you ladies held shit down you were doing business with the Russians with a mutual understanding. Now I have word that they have partnered with Vito, Derrick and Jim. Shit's different now. It's not just the Russians we have to worry about. Collectively they're calling themselves the Russian Cartel."

I stood up and took a deep breath. Stuffing my hands into my fatigue pants my mind wandered for a moment. For some reason, I imagined Kevin being with another woman and I wanted to snatch his face off his skull. Instead I brought my thoughts back to business and said, "Russian Cartel or not, they can still be brought down."

"You saying the same thing, Bambi," Kevin replied. "Anything can happen if we close our eyes and imagine," he chuckled. "But this is not make believe. This is war."

"You're right, husband. And the last time I heard, I was the only one in this room who served time on the battlefield. If you were in my platoon you would be reporting to me, soldier. So where's my salute?"

I heard Race and Scarlett giggle.

"Let me remind you of something that I think is important," I continued. "Before I was a Kennedy, I was in the US Army. That means I defended not only America but also every last nigga in this room. And if there was one thing I learned it was the art of war." I paused. "So what is my resolution? We bring them down by first dismantling their soldiers and any help they may have. Like they're trying to do ours."

"And then?" Camp said.

"We kill the Russians swiftly and without remorse."

Kevin looked at me in silence. In fact, the room was so quiet you could hear blood pumping through their veins. When I looked at the fellas they didn't seem excited about my idea. But each one of my sisters looked at me with grins on their faces.

If I had their support, I was good.

"You can't be serious," Kevin responded. "Who are we going to use to go at the Russians? We are losing five percent of our soldiers every week. Race just told you that. With the exception of the men guarding this property, we out of manpower."

"We get the east coast bosses involved. We bring them here and stress the importance of banding together."

"But you reached out to them already," he replied. "And since the Russians are not directly threatening them they told you to beat it. Why do you think that would change?"

"Because I will give them a threat. One they can't ignore."

"Meaning?" Bradley said. He was no longer massaging Denim's shoulders. Now his attention was on me.

Where it belonged.

"When Sarge gets back from handling business in Mexico for Mitch we'll use a few of his men. He has access to about fifty of them. Then we give them a command to kill a few key people in the east coast bosses' organizations and blame it on the Russians. This will bring them to their knees and then I'll call them again with another option to band together. I'm sure they'll pledge allegiance at that time."

"How do you know this will work?" Camp questioned.

"Trust me, it will. I believe they already know that this Russian shit can trickle downhill. This will give them the permission they need to make a move. With us."

Kevin laughed hysterically. "Do you know how ridiculous you sound?" He paused. "You talking about killing Russians who have supporters in other countries you know nothing of."

I stared at him with pity. "Why are you scared? You are more powerful than them and yet you can't even see it," I said. "But when I look at you I see a boss, which is why I agreed to be your wife. If they were as solid as you claim they wouldn't want the nigga downstairs so badly." I paused. "We have Mitch so we have the drug industry."

"This is a dangerous plan," Bradley said. "Have we weighed the cost?"

I rolled my eyes. This nigga was always talking about money.

"What did you gentlemen think I meant when I said we were at war?" I asked skipping the subject. "That we were about to play the board game Battleship?"

"Don't be disrespectful," Kevin shouted slamming his fist into the table, temporarily stopping my heart.

"This is not about respect. It's about moves." I paused. "And if you don't like my plan, counter it with a better one."

"Come on, Bambi," Bradley said. "Slow down."

"I'm serious! Ya'll act like ya'll want us to stay holed up in here while they bring down everything we worked so hard for in the outside world." I paused. "This place is sweet but what happens when the cash runs out? And we don't have enough money to pay the soldiers? Bradley, you always talking about paper but what about that?"

He nodded.

"I mean we're good for at least ten years if you consider food and supplies but if we hide out forever, what does that make us?" I continued.

"Cowards," Denim responded.

"I'm not saying that we should stay here forever," Bradley replied. "I just want to make sure shit works."

"It will work but I need the support of our family." I looked at everyone. "Say that you'll help me. Say that you sanction my moves because I can't do this without ya'll."

Kevin looked around at everyone. "Well let's put it to a vote," Kevin said. "Who here is with Bambi's plan?"

Race, Scarlett and Denim raised their hands instantly and I winked. Camp looked at Kevin and Bradley but he pushed his hand up too, followed by Bradley and Ramirez.

With everyone in agreement, we all looked at Kevin. "I guess it doesn't matter what I choose," he responded walking away without weighing in.

"I hope this will work," Camp said. "For all of our sake."

"It will work. Trust me."

I walked into Kevin's room and hung in the doorway. "I can't believe after everything I've done to keep this family going that I still don't have your support."

He moved the pillows to the other side of the bed, pulled down the comforter and sat on the edge of the mattress to take off his shoes. "What do you want, boss? The family is on your side. Isn't that enough?"

By T. Styles

I wanted to say no. I wanted to tell him how much I needed his support but pride would not allow me. "I don't trust Mitch," I said skipping the subject.

He looked up at me.

Now I had the nigga's attention.

"Bambi, you already have a lot on your plate with the Russians. Don't go and get us all killed by doing something to Mitch."

"Who said I was going to harm him?"

"I can see it in your eyes. He's our connect, Bambi. And if your plan works, nothing we do matters if he's gone." He paused. "Because contrary to what you believe, Mitch is the drug industry."

I smiled at him and turned around.

"Bambi! Bambi," he yelled as I ignored him and walked down the hall. "Bambi, are you listening to me?"

CHAPTER TWELVE
DENIM

After the meeting and talking to Bambi and Race, I walked into the large kitchen to get a sandwich. My mother sat at the table with a box of donuts in front of her and the rim of the milk glass pressed against her lips. She placed it down and thumbed through an Essence Magazine sitting in front of her. "So what was the meeting about?" she asked me before flipping another page.

I grabbed a water bottle from the fridge, slogged toward the table and flopped down next to her. "Nothing you need to worry about." I twisted the cap off and took a swig.

"Then how come I'm hearing the word Russian brought up every five minutes in this house?" She closed the magazine and grabbed another donut. Stuffing it into the center of her jaw, white powder sat in the corners of her mouth as she chomped.

"Mama, right now I'm not in the mood." I took another sip of water and laid my head on the table. I was sicker than ever and it felt as if I had the flu.

"Tell me something I don't know," she responded with her mouth full.

"You're safe here, mama. Trust me. Nobody knows where this place is and even if they did, you can't get past the soldiers we have surrounding the property." I paused and put my forehead back on the cool table. "You can't even use a cell phone except the one we assigned you on the property."

"I know. That's why ya'll gave me this bullshit ass phone," she said sliding her Samsung Galaxy S5 across the table.

"That's a five hundred dollar phone, ma." I gave her a new phone because I wanted her to stay away from her old crowd. I destroyed the other one and claimed I lost it.

"But it's not mine. Now I have to try and remember all of my friends' numbers and give them my new one. Ya'll cutting me off at the legs."

"Mama, please," I said, not feeling like arguing with her. "Can't you see that I don't feel well?" I paused. "I just want to relax."

"Have you told him yet?" she asked stuffing another powdered donut in her mouth. "That you not having the baby?"

"Who said I'm not having my child?"

"You would be stupid to have that baby. You don't need that shit right—"

"Why you talking to my wife so recklessly?" Bradley asked stomping into the kitchen. His fists were clenched as he approached my mother from behind. "Huh? Didn't I warn you about that shit?"

When I saw his face I stood up and blocked his path. This was the second time he looked like he wanted to do my mother harm and it was making me nervous. Placing my hands on his chest, I said, "Baby, come with me to our room."

I felt his body soften but his gaze remained fixated on my mother. "I want you to stop putting bullshit in my wife's head." He placed his hand on my belly. "This my baby in her body and you don't have a say so about what we do."

"Nigga, I don't care about that shit!" my mother snapped. "You killed my child," she paused, "and now I want to kill yours."

My heart stopped when I heard my mother's hateful words. I turned around and faced her. "What the fuck do you mean by that shit, mama?"

The anger washed off her face and guilt replaced it. "Nothing, I was just...I was..."

Bradley grabbed my shoulders and looked at me. Tears rolled down my cheek as I realized my mother was trying to get me to abort my baby just to hurt Bradley.

"I told you, Denim," Bradley said softly. "Your mother is here to try and ruin us." I was still looking at her until he raised my chin so that my gaze fell on him. "Don't you see that? Are you going to stand by and allow her to destroy everything we built?"

I looked at my mother and my stomach rumbled with disgust and rage.

"Either she goes or I do," he said to me. "Make a decision soon, Denim. Because if you don't, I'll make it for you." He walked out and I felt heavy.

"Don't listen to him, Denim," my mother said softly. "He's just—"

"Fuck you, bitch!"

I stomped out of the kitchen and down the corridor before she could finish her sentence. I was sick of her. Sick of him. And sick of the Russians.

I needed to get away from her. I needed to take in what was happening around me.

As I walked aimlessly down the hallway, for the first time I took a real look at the design of our new home. The bunker was beautiful but there were so many rooms it was easy to get lost within the walls.

When I finally made it to my room I plopped on my bed, not knowing Bambi was behind me. "You heard the argument?" I asked.

"Yes," she responded.

"I don't want to talk about it right now," I replied.

"You going to hear what I have to say whether you want to or not," she said. "I know you love your mother. I love mine too. But I'll be damned if I let her come in the way of my marriage." She paused. "Bradley is right, Denim. He's also right for you. So if he says your mother has to go then maybe you should listen."

"I'm not feeling Bradley right now, Bambi. And I know you know that."

She sighed. "I know it's fucked up. But once we make a decision on who we choose to be in our lives, we have to stick to it. We have to honor it. Being a Kennedy ain't for everybody."

"You should listen to your own advice with Kevin."

"That's different," she sighed. "We talking about you and the fact that it's probably not a good idea for your mother to stay here anymore. All she's doing is stirring up shit at the wrong time."

"But what if the Russians get to her?"

"We got money, Denim. It's nothing for us to put her somewhere where they can't get to her."

"But what if she doesn't stay? I'll be worried sick."

"You already had the other house you bought her bulldozed down so she can't go back to that nasty mothafucka. That's the last house the Russians knew about. She doesn't have a job so they can't get her there. She has no choice but to stay where you put her."

"I'll think about it," I said rubbing my throbbing temples. Everything on my body seemed to ache. "Until then, I need you to get one of Sarge's men to take me into the city."

"For what?"

"To have an abortion."

CHAPTER THIRTEEN
BAMBI

I felt relaxed as I sat in our living room and talked to Quartz, one of Sarge's soldiers. He was there to have an audience with Mitch and advise him on Sarge's progress in Mexico. Sarge was there to handle the day-to-day operations for Mitch since he couldn't physically be there.

Make no mistake, although Sarge may have been managing the cocaine crops in Mexico, it was Mitch who was running the show. Sarge didn't do a thing without his approval.

After speaking to Mitch, Quartz sat with me to give me an update. Although this was business, I couldn't help but notice how Quartz looked at me. His light brown skin glowed and his hazel eyes seemed to peer through my soul. He'd always looked upon me that way, even before I had a bigger hand in the operation.

A lot of men find women in power sexually attractive but today I noticed him too. Maybe it was Kevin's betrayal or maybe it was just the man before me.

Who knows?

And who cares?

Whatever it was, for the moment, I decided to give him my undivided eye.

"Mitch looks good," Quartz said as he leaned back in the large, plush leather sofa. "And I know he wants to be back in Mexico but you're taking good care of him here." His eyes rolled away from mine, down to my thighs that were laced in a pair of tight jeans and then up at my eyes again. "I see you're taking care of yourself too." He licked his lips and

By T. Styles

looked at me seductively. "Then again, you always do."

"Why would you come at me like that?" I snapped as if I were highly offended.

The smug expression on his face wiped off.

"I'm your boss, Quartz. Not the other way around." Although I was bored and willing to spend some time with him, I wanted him to know that I was in control. *Always.* Any attention I gave him would be an honor, not a privilege.

He exhaled and said, "I'm sorry, Bambi." He didn't seem frazzled by my sternness and that made him more appealing. "I meant no disrespect. Sometimes I say what's on my mind without thinking. But it won't happen again."

He stood up to leave and moved toward the front door.

I crossed my legs and said, "I didn't dismiss you yet, soldier." He turned around. "Have a seat until I do so."

He swaggered back toward me and did as instructed. With a grin on his face, he said, "You look good in power."

"I look good in everything I do," I winked.

He laughed.

"Can I offer you a drink?" I asked.

"Not if I can't speak freely around you, Mrs. Kennedy."

"Meaning?"

"Meaning I'm attracted to you. If you didn't know before, you know now." He paused. "And unless I can say what's on my mind, I'm going to have to respectfully request that you allow me to leave. Liquor makes me more comfortable and I don't want to offend you again. Besides, I've already done that."

I smiled at him, stood up and walked over to the fully equipped bar. I could feel his eyes on my ass because my pussy throbbed. I poured myself a glass of wine and splashed a couple shots of cognac in a glass for him. Switching back over to the couch, I handed him his drink and I sipped my wine. "You can speak freely, Quartz. As long as you make it interesting."

Three hours passed and Quartz and I were laughing it up. I realized we had more in common than I originally thought. I learned that prior to the dope game, he was in the military like I was. So he understood the lifestyle and how sometimes you can come back mentally fucked up due to some of the things you saw over there.

He was divorced, single and throwing himself into his work to relieve stress. And I was married, overworked and lonely. I was having such a good time that I didn't realize Kevin was standing at the table looking at us.

When did he get there?

He wasn't home earlier and since the night was still young, I didn't expect to see him until later on.

"What's this?" he asked with a frown on his face. When I looked down at Kevin's hands I saw that his fists were clenched.

"Hey, man," Quartz said standing up with a smile on his face. He outstretched his hand for Kevin to shake it but Kevin refused. Quartz cleared his throat, tucked both hands in his pockets and said, "Maybe I should leave."

"I'll talk to you later," I said as he walked toward the door in a hurry.

"No you won't," Kevin interrupted. "Slow your roll, Mrs. Kennedy. Your company is leaving the building."

This nigga Kevin was mad funny. Here he was standing up in my face like he hadn't been doing him with some random bitch for the past few weeks.

And now he wanted to stunt me?

Quartz nodded and walked out.

When he was gone I thought Kevin was about to argue with me. Instead, he gripped me by my throat and ushered me to the bathroom directly off of the living room. I didn't fight with him because the pleasure I received from seeing his anger told me that I already won the battle.

I didn't mention his bitch he was with and yet he got a taste of his own medicine.

Once we were there, he pushed me toward the sink and turned me around. One hand pressed against each side of the sink. I was now facing myself in the mirror as my husband snatched down my jeans and fucked me from the back.

It hurt due to the amount of pressure he was putting on me but my pussy didn't know there was drama in my marriage. The rage mixed with his jealousy caused me to get wet. If I didn't care about him this would feel like rape, which technically it was. But because I knew I still wanted to be with him even though I didn't want to admit it, I enjoyed every minute of it.

When he was done he pulled out of me and looked at me through the mirror. He placed his lips on my shoulder and I thought he was about to kiss me. Instead, he bit me and before I could scream out, he slammed his dry hand over my lips. "Don't get that nigga killed, soldier." He pulled his pants up. "Don't get yourself killed too. The next nigga you allow inside of you will die there. I promise."

He walked out of the bathroom, leaving me alone.

Soaking in the tub, I was trying to get Kevin's cum out of my body. I never knew it was possible to hate and love a nigga in the same breath and yet I did.

The place where he bit into my flesh still throbbed even though he didn't break my skin.

I was thinking about Kevin. I was thinking about Denim's recent abortion and what it would do to her marriage. But the most dominating thought above all was this beef with the Russians.

Larry was causing more problems in my organization than I could stand. He managed to kill a few more key people in our empire and their loved ones. A man like this did not deserve to be on the streets.

I needed a specialized killer, one who was not on the Russians' radar. Yet Race had failed to come through.

When my phone vibrated and I saw it was Race, I answered. "What's up?" I winced a little in pain.

"I think I found who you need," she said. I could tell she was smiling.

I sat up in the tub quickly, pushing some water outside of the tub in the process. "Where are you?"

"I'm at a diner. But trust me, I do have the right person."

"What's his name?"

"He is a she."

I leaned back in the tub and smiled. "Well I can't wait to meet her."

After ending the call with her, I decided to make another one. It rang once before being answered.

"Is this my beautiful Bambi Kennedy?" Arkadi said as if he were happy to hear from me.

"And to think, I wasn't sure if you would remember my number," I crossed my legs in the tub.

"To what do I owe this call?" He paused. "Are you and the other Kennedys ready to submit to me? And be the good little niggers I know you can be."

I laughed, grabbed the washcloth and scrubbed my pussy clean. "You didn't get the memo? We're free now."

He chuckled. "What the fuck do you want?"

"I actually have one question for you. What made you send your girlfriend over to my home, when you knew we could've killed her?"

"It was same reason you allowed her to leave. I wanted to fuck with your head. And since you packed up and left, I guess I've done that."

I nodded. "I love her face, Arkadi. With the exception of the black eye you left."

"That's more than I can say for you."

"This is true," I nodded. "Which is why I wanted to call you first. To let you know that soon, very soon, I will see to it that a hole is blown in her face so large that there won't be a thing left you recognize about her. Including her beauty."

CHAPTER FOURTEEN
RACE
THREE HOURS EARLIER

I don't even know what I was doing in Smack Back Strip Club, the place Carey used to work. The place where I first met her.

When I realized that I drank so much that I could barely hold my head up, I knew it was time to bounce. Suddenly the dark club and the loud music felt creepy to me.

What was I doing there?

I was Race Kennedy of the Pretty Kings. And I had a hit on my head by the Russians.

Leaving a few bills on the table, slowly I rose, grabbed my car keys and left the club. I was almost to my car when I heard a male voice say, "Don't scream."

When I turned around I saw the clenched teeth of a man I didn't know. Who was this nigga who thought he was bold enough to rob me? When I could lay hands on him and every person he ever loved?

"You coming with me and you'll live as long as you don't make any crazy moves," he continued.

I might have been shorter than him but I wasn't scared as I looked up into his eyes. I knew a punk when I saw one. If I had my hammer I would've brought him to his knees. But when I left out of the bunker tonight I wasn't thinking straight and now I was bare. "Do you know who I am?" I asked calmly.

"Why else would I—"

His sentence was severed suddenly when I saw a hand placed over his mouth. I was in awe as I witnessed a silver blade slide across his throat slowly, causing the pinkness of his flesh to spill out like cream.

I could've sworn I heard her say, "Goon."

When his body dropped, I was staring up into the green eyes of a tall, beautiful woman. I noticed her in the strip club a few times when I was there to visit Carey. I thought she kept time with Carey but I couldn't be sure. I knew she was a dancer but never a killer and suddenly I was intrigued.

"Figured you could use the help," she said with a glistening red knife in her hand.

"That's what I call perfect timing," I responded.

The air conditioner was on too high in the small diner we were sitting in. I was trying to get to know the talented killer who saved my life but she was proving to be tough as rawhide.

It was as if she didn't trust me.

After she killed him, we tucked his body in my trunk like trash. Then I called Sarge, who just got back from Mexico, for added assistance. He was my right hand in the underworld of our operation and in less than fifteen minutes, he had two carloads of loyal soldiers on the scene with one mission in mind, to make the corpse disappear.

I realized I was slipping big time after I almost lost my life and suddenly my buzz was gone. Now sober, I wanted to know more about the woman who killed so easily. The woman who kept me breathing with one slash of her weapon.

With skills like that, the chick I now knew as Roman could be of great use to our squad. Being female would give her access to places that Sarge and the other soldiers couldn't roam.

She was the perfect killer Bambi was looking for.

A cup of coffee sat in front of Roman and a cup of water with lemon was before me. A respectful power struggle occurred as we attempted to get to know one another. She didn't seem moved by my power even though I was sure she knew who I was.

"Where is Carey?" Roman asked flatly. "I'm looking for her." She took a sip of coffee.

I wasn't expecting to hear her name. My head hung low and I decided to lie. "I don't know. That's why I was in the club tonight. I talk to Carey every day and all of a sudden she's not returning my calls. It's been fucking my head up." I sipped my water. "So tell me...were you two close?"

"Extremely," she responded. "Like sisters."

I moved uneasily in my seat. Where was my confidence? "Did she tell you anything about me?"

"Not really," she said as she seemed to be looking through me. "Just that she had a bond with you and your husband. Which I was leery about but respected."

She seemed to be holding back a little as if she didn't trust me.

"I took care of her," I responded. I wanted to be honest without being totally truthful. "We paid for her house, her car and her luxuries. I loved her very much. Me and my husband." I rubbed my hand down my face. "I know people might not understand our brand of love but it worked for us, you know?"

Roman shrugged. "I don't judge."

"I figured as much," I smiled. "Look, I asked you here for a reason. The way you got rid of that nigga tonight was amazing. I've met killers before. *Many.* But your moves were calculated." I paused. "I have a place for someone of your skill set in my operation. That is, if you want it."

"Are you asking if I'm interested in murder for hire?"

"Yes."

Silence.

Without responding, Roman looked toward her right, out of the window with several people walking by. When I followed her gaze I saw a little girl, who was certainly up past her bedtime, skipping along with her family. While the young black couple held hands, the little girl chased the leash to the collar that was wrapped around her dog's neck.

After looking at the scene, Roman took a deep breath and said, "I'm sorry, Race." She paused. "I'm glad you're safe. But the life you are offering is not for me anymore."

So she was a killer who chose to retire.

I reached into my purse and said, "Well let me give you something for your—"

"No." Roman shook her head when she saw I was handing her money. "Consider his death a gift from me to you. I hated that nigga." She stood up and smiled. "Good luck." She walked out, but not without me slipping my card in her pocket.

The fact that she played hard to get made me want to be in contact with her even more. I was sure I'd see her again and I knew we would do business. But first, I had to call Bambi and tell her the partial good news.

A WEEK LATER

I was right. Not even a week later, Roman sat in the middle of the floor on a leather recliner inside of the bunker.

My sisters all stood before her. Bambi stepped away from us wearing her green fatigue pants and a black t-shirt. She only wore her fatigues when she meant business.

Roman was dressed in all black. Black pants and a black hoodie. The darkness of her gear set off her green eyes.

"My name is Bambi Kennedy," she said. "And you are here because Race has told me great things about you." She walked closer and stopped before dipping into Roman's personal space. "I don't know what we would have done if she would've died. I do know the city would have been red with blood." She paused. "I appreciate your diligence. We need people like you on our team."

Roman remained quiet.

"We have an issue with a recent enemy who has moved into our territory," Bambi continued. "Having worthy soldiers is not an issue for my organization. I command a huge team of killers who are able-bodied and ready."

"So what is the concern?"

"We need someone who can act as a chameleon. A person who can move around easily without being spotted. One with experience." She paused. "Before I go any further, I must know something. And I would appreciate your candor."

"What is it?" Roman asked.

"Are you the one they call Goon? From Baltimore? The one who seemed to disappear without ever getting caught, leaving a trail of bodies behind?"

Roman looked guilty and I had my answer. I couldn't believe we lucked up like this. Bambi had been trying to find her and I always thought she was an urban legend. Now I see it is not true.

"If I told you, then you'd know more than is necessary."

Bambi laughed but she looked satisfied with Roman's response. "Before I saw you, and your height, I knew Goon was a woman. Only a woman could keep a secret this long and get away with it. Men often require the credit for such acts. So they boast. But you don't."

Roman smiled at the compliment but remained poised. "Who do you need done?" she asked plainly.

"It's not necessarily who but how many."

"I'm listening."

"Before we get into that, let's talk about what you desire."

"What makes you think I desire anything?"

"We all want something, Roman. And I'm told that you have needs that we may be able to meet."

Roman sighed. I didn't know her home situation but I knew she wanted to help her dude. I think he was in college or some shit like that and couldn't pay the tuition. That's the only thing she told me.

"I need money. For my husband."

"And we have plenty," Bambi assured her.

"But he can't know what I'm doing. This has to remain anonymous."

"I respect anonymity," Bambi nodded. "And we never get involved in personal affairs, even if we become enemies." She paused. "I'm about money. And since we're on that issue, what is your fee?"

"Twenty-five thousand dollars."

When I heard her amount, I busted out laughing. She must have been used to rolling with broke bitches if she asked for so little cash. I guess dancing on the pole couldn't allow her to see bigger. But she was fucking with the big girls now.

"What's funny?" Roman asked.

"Roman, for the people we need you to murder, we are willing to pay you one million dollars," Bambi responded.

Roman's eyes widened upon hearing our proposal. I bet she never dreamed of making so much money. We didn't mind paying out when necessary, especially for a job like this. And especially when women were involved. We believed in looking out for each other at all times.

Roman adjusted uneasily in her seat. Now her cool manner seemed to be gone. We officially won her over.

"Excuse me...did you say a million?" Roman asked.

"You heard me correctly," Bambi confirmed. "I don't want you to knock over a few dope boys. We have a squad for that. The people I'm seeking your assistance for have caused major problems for my organization. So they require care and confidentiality. You demonstrated that when you killed back in the day and maintained your silence...even now. Mellvue, the girlfriend of our biggest enemy, has family in the area and she won't be as easy to get as the others. Her movements are sporadic and he takes care to protect her."

"I understand. But I will need help."

"You can use some of our men."

"I'm sorry, Bambi. But in order for me to do this properly, I need to work with men I trust. I hope that's okay."

Bambi looked at me and I nodded in approval.

"We will have Sarge run a background check on the men you've chosen," Bambi continued. "If they come back clean I'm okay with that."

"A million dollars is a lot of money," Roman replied. "Just for a few people."

Bambi walked closer and looked down at her. "I know, Roman. A million dollars is hefty." She paused. "That's why I must tell you. For the money, you will owe me a hundred lives."

She nodded and said, "Who do you want me to get first."

"Larry of the Reapers. I need this nigga killed like yesterday."

"Consider it done."

LARRY – THE REAPERS

"Somebody's shooting!" screeched a paunchy woman as she gripped her lower belly while charging through the mall. Turning around momentarily to see if the killer was upon her, her eyes widened when she witnessed a tidal wave of terror-stricken people zooming in her direction. Her heart thrashed against the walls of her chest just as her high heeled shoe failed, causing her to plummet against the grungy floor, slamming on her knees a bit too roughly. When a pain she hadn't expected sequenced through her ankle she looked down only to see the bloody bone projecting

through the flesh of her lower leg. "Help me! Please, somebody!" she begged with an outstretched hand.

The thing was this. The horde was unmerciful and it was each man for himself. Some leaped over her, while others stepped on her limbs in an attempt to survive.

More gunfire blazed through the gallery as another woman screamed. "God, help us all! What's happening?" Each time shots echoed throughout the air, it would give the weary dynamism to push harder. To run faster.

When the herd of souls reached a fork in the mall, some advanced right while others moved left, including a spry drug dealer and an old man who needed assistance from a cherry wood cane, else he would be trampled like the woman some feet back.

Proceeding in the same direction, they both continued their search for freedom when the elderly man happened upon a beige door with a white and black sign marked Employees Only. Seeking sanctuary, his wrinkled hand covered the doorknob when suddenly the inconsiderate drug dealer shoved him to the side as if he were going into his own home.

Although youthful, his skin was bumpy and his broad forehead was contracted in rage so that his eyebrows formed an inky line. "Get out my way, old man! Before I burn your ass down." He raised his shirt, showing his .45. With warnings in the air, he slipped inside thinking of his own protection.

Fortunately for the elder, he was able to make it into the darkness with his younger counterpart just before he slammed the door and the sounds of gunfire grew nearer.

More shots fired.

More screaming voices.

The reign of terror seemed endless.

When the senior stepped on the drug dealer's toe as he struggled to get situated, he pushed him back roughly. "Move the fuck out of my way," he whispered harshly. The senior was knocked into the brooms on the back wall, causing a shooting pain down his spine. Neither could see the other's eyes but they could feel the tension in the tight space. "Step on my J's again and I'ma crack your fucking jaw," he whispered, stabbing a stiff finger in the middle of his chest.

"S-sorry," the old man responded, his voice quavering.

With the matter out of the way, they focused on the closed door again and the screaming from the people outside. The young dealer was hopeful that he might make it out alive until he heard the senior's rough breathing that whistled slightly as he inhaled and exhaled. The dealer was certain that if the gunman was near, he would hear the elder and this made him uncomfortable. He would've thrown him out but what if the gunman saw him? Both of them may have been killed.

In panic mode, he turned around again. He was certainly tiring of the old geezer. So he gripped the collar of the senior's shirt. Removing his weapon, he touched the cool steel to his nose and growled, "Either you stop breathing or I'll stop it for you." He cocked his bird. "What you wanna do?"

"I'll...I'll try to be quiet," he stuttered. "Please don't kill me."

"Good choice," the dealer responded before shoving him back into the wall and aiming at the door, ready to fire at whoever came inside. He deduced that the shooter was some crazed white boy, mad at the world and the parents who brought him into it.

The older man continued to breathe heavily until his respiration ceased abruptly, along with the noise outside. There was no wind down or fade out. As if the mayhem in and out of the closet never existed, it was eerily silent. The type of silence that birthed insecurity and fear.

Suddenly the skills the young dealer adapted on the streets—the ones that kept him alive even though he was a most hated man, due to the nights he and his crew, the Reapers, robbed competitors of their stashes—kicked in.

"You know now, don't you?" the senior whispered closely into his ear. His voice was different but vaguely the same. "That I'm here for you."
When the dealer tried to fire at the old man the warm palm of the senior's hand pressed against his wind-pipe while his other hand now secured a knife at the dealer's neck. "Don't turn around," he demanded. "I'm very swift."

Suddenly the recollection became apparent.

He was a she.

"What did I do?" He was certain she was some bit-ter bitch he fucked who went through amazing odds to get even by causing a diversion in the mall. "At least tell me who you are!"

Without responding, in the blink of an eye, the elder-turned-Impaler pressed the blade deeper into his throat, past the skin, past the arteries and through the cartilage until it could go no further. Warm blood oozed over her fingers and splashed to the floor.

Although he was helpless and no longer a threat, the Impaler held onto the dealer's body until she felt his spirit exit this world. When he went limp, she placed her lips against his earlobe again and whis-pered, "Goon."

CHAPTER FIFTEEN
ARKADI LENIN

*A*rkadi sat in an old wooden chair in the basement of the hideout he shared with his brother. A carton of eggs sat on his lap and he picked one up and held it firmly in his hand.

Across from him was Mellvue, his fiancé. She was sitting in a large trashcan with ropes wrapped around her arms, preventing her from moving her limbs. Although she was stuffed inside of it, he hadn't bothered to empty the garbage contents prior to her placement. He wanted to humiliate her as he always did whenever he was angry and drunk.

And now he was furious.

Bambi had successfully knocked one of the legs from up under their operation by killing Larry of the Reapers. She was smarter than even he gave her credit for and as a result, he chose to bathe in his rage by abusing his beautiful fiancé.

He raised the egg and tossed it at Mellvue. It smacked dead in the middle of her forehead. Yolk mixed with blood rolled down her face.

"Arkadi, please," she cried. "I'm sorry for speaking harshly to you. Still, I don't understand why you would treat me like this. Why you would humiliate me?"

He removed another egg, sat the carton on the floor and picked up his glass before walking over to Mellvue. When he reached her he slammed the egg down on her face. Then he swallowed the rest of the vodka in the glass, tossed it in the can with her and then undid his pants.

She looked up at what he was doing and he re-leased his penis. Holding it in his hand, he urinated on her head. When he was done he lowered his head and slapped her in the face.

Her neck cracked and her spine throbbed.

"If you disobey me again and leave my house without making your whereabouts known, I will kill you." He paused. "Do you understand why?"

She nodded and tried to suppress the tears that wanted to pour from her soul. "Yes."

"Tell me."

"Because you don't want anything happening to me."

He laughed. "On the contrary, that is least of my concerns." He paused. "I don't want the Kennedys thinking they got over on me by getting to you. So do what I say. And stay the fuck off streets. Or I will send you back to Russia where you belong."

CHAPTER SIXTEEN
SCARLETT
TWO WEEKS LATER

Earlier, Detective Morris Swanson called and told me he wanted to ask me some questions about our case. When I asked Camp was he going to the appointment with me, he said he was helping to prepare the bunker for the east coast bosses' arrival in a few days and couldn't go. But he was aware of our meeting.

For some reason, I felt as if this day would come, where I would be alone with the man whose focus was exposing my secrets. But there was no way around it. I had to go. I needed to find out how much he discovered.

In his office, I sat in a raggedy black chair and picked up a four-year-old magazine from the glass table. I was nervous and when his secretary, a twenty-something-year-old black girl with a large butt, came out to get me I was startled.

"He'll see you now," she said as she popped the gum in her mouth and rolled her eyes.

I tossed the magazine on the table, stood up and said, "Where?"

"Go on in the back. You'll see the door marked Morris Swanson. That is, if you can read."

I followed the rude bitch's directions and walked toward the office. She'd better be glad my temper was easier than Bambi or Race's.

I was the quiet one. The one who didn't use violence first. Because if I did, I may have placed a call to have her dealt with later.

When I made it to the back I noticed his office was the same place where I first met him so I should've remembered.

I walked in and sat on the other side of his desk but he wasn't there and I was irritated. When my cell phone rang I saw it was Race and answered. "What's up?" I asked looking around.

There was a picture on his desk. He had his arm around his rude secretary and she was pregnant in the photo. I guess they were together.

Gross!

"You know the girl we have working on the file?" she asked.

I knew she was talking about Roman who was hired to kill key members in our organization who stepped out of line, and many more in the east coast bosses' operations so that they could see that the Russian threat was real.

"Yeah, did she get the main client yet?" I asked, referring to Mellvue.

"No," she sighed. "But I know she's on it. She's sick with it, Scarlett," she said excitedly. "Already handled Felicia's hating ass from the Southeast Kittens and Larry at Mondawmin Mall," Race continued excitedly. Mellvue is still alive but I think over time, she will prove to be a good investment."

I smiled hoping in the long run this Russian business would be behind us so that we could get back to enjoying each other. To spending quality time together. Everything felt so tense now. "So what can I do?"

"Well she has something going on in her personal life. She needs a white girl to pretend to be her boss at work. To make her look good."

My eyes widened because I wasn't expecting her to say anything like that. I wasn't naive. I knew that

By T. Styles

some people in my race perceived themselves and other white people as superior.

But I didn't.

I never had my family make a request to use me for my skin color until now. It didn't bother me though. If I could help them, I would.

"She got a full time job?" I asked, surprised someone who was given a million would still be working.

"No, we got to set everything up in this building she rented like she does have a job." She paused. "I think she's trying to throw her husband off so that he doesn't know what she really does for a living. Normally I wouldn't waste my time with bullshit but I need all obstacles to be out of this chick's way so she can do her job and Bambi can stay off my back."

"So what is my part in all of this?"

"When I give you the word I need you to go to the building. Just answer any questions her husband or anybody else has so that things can go smoothly. We need some girls though to be your employees."

"Okay, I'll pay a few chicks who lookout for the cops for us in Morgan Projects."

"Make it worth their while, Scarlett."

"I'll give them five hundred dollars apiece for a week to just hang out there. If Roman's husband pops up when I'm not there, I want him to see that things are running smoothly. And when you call me I'll go there too."

"No doubt," she said excitedly. She gave me all of the information and I grabbed a piece of paper and pen off of Swanson's desk to write things down. Before I hung up, she asked, "Are you okay, Scarlett?"

I exhaled. "As okay as I'm going to be," I said as I looked back at the door wondering where Morris was.

"Just know that I'm here. I might not agree with how you handling my little shawty but it is your decision. Besides, I been over there and you right, the family looks legit. I can tell they really love the kid."

With raised brows, I asked, "You've been over there already?"

"I only been twice," she laughed. "Denim been every day since she got the information."

I shook my head. Denim was going to be a problem.

"I just wanted you to know that you're not alone," she continued.

Just as Swanson was walking in, I responded, "I know, Race. Thank you."

When I got off the phone with her, I addressed him. "You called me here so what's up?"

Instead of answering me, he walked behind his desk, pulled open a drawer and tossed a manila folder on top of it. "Open it."

Slowly I reached for the folder and skimmed through the contents. My heart dropped. Everything I thought I ran away from in my past was inside. He had information about my daughter, the charges for child abuse. My parents' names, my racist brother, everything was in the folder before me. And in the back he had a picture of the Walkers with Master clutched in Mrs. Walker's arms.

I dropped the folder on the floor. With tears rolling down my face, I asked, "What do you want?"

"No need to cry, redhead." He smiled. "I'll call you with my fee. Just be ready to deliver."

By T. Styles

My knees were close to my chest and I was looking at Camp who was wearing another t-shirt with Master's face.

It was weird.

Master was bigger now and didn't even look the same, yet Camp still sported the same t-shirt, getting new ones made every week.

He just got off the phone with Swanson who said the case was looking hopeful. And that he would call him very soon with more information.

Things were about to blow up in my face.

I had one question to ask myself. Should I take Master away from the Walkers so that they'd never see him again or tell my husband the truth?

I didn't know what to do.

"C...Camp," I stuttered. "Have you given any more thought to us being together and working on our marriage?"

He exhaled and sat on the edge of his bed and put on his shoes. "Honey, the only thing on my mind right now is finding our son. I hate to be cold but it's true."

I held my head down. "I know, Camp. And I'm trying not to be selfish. I just want to know that if we find Master...I mean when we find Master, I want to make sure that you will still be here for me." I paused. "I've given you your space. I stay out of your way and I've even stopped asking about our marriage. Hasn't that told you that I've changed?"

"Scarlett, the only thing time apart has shown me is that I can do well without you. So while I appreciate it, it's not working to your advantage."

My head dropped and he moved closer to me and placed his hands on the sides of my face. It was the first time in a long time that he touched me. "I know hearing this shit hurts, which is why I didn't want to talk about it, Scarlett. I just want you to know that I will not leave your side until Master is found. We are a team and when we find our son that still won't change. We still have to raise him together and as his mother, I will always love you."

A tear fell from his eye and dropped on my face. I wondered if the tears were for me or Master. No matter what, I could feel the love pouring from his body.

He pulled me in and hugged me tightly within his arms. I inhaled his expensive cologne and exhaled slowly. "I'm going to find our son, Scarlett." He kissed the top of my head. "I promise you."

I knew he was right and that's what scared me the most.

CHAPTER SEVENTEEN
DENIM

Helping Bambi place dinner plates on the large table in the dining room, my mind was flooded. The east coast bosses were coming and one from down south was also on the way.

Although important, I wasn't feeling the meeting because Bradley and I were at odds but I knew there was a time and place for everything.

Bambi wore a huge smile on her face as she got things prepared and I wondered why she was so happy. "What's on your mind?" I asked. "You awfully excited, considering our troubles."

"Mellvue's dead," she grinned. "That bitch walked up in our house and now we put her out her misery right along with Larry."

"Are you serious?" I asked hopefully.

"Yes! Roman is vicious! And the best part about it is it happened right before the meeting with the bosses. Now I can tell them that we've fired a shot at them in their honor. Considering they've all lost good men, this will be good news."

With Roman on the streets, Bambi was successfully able to kill a few key members in each east coast boss's organization and now they considered the Russians to be a threat.

With part one of her plan out of the way, Bambi sent cars to pick everyone up since the bunker was off the map and couldn't be located in any other way. Now we were just waiting for them to trickle inside.

I smiled and focused back on the table. "That's a relief."

"That was extra dry," Bambi responded.

"I'm sorry, Bambi. My head is all over the place."

"What's on your mind?" Bambi asked placing a fork next to a plate.

"Bambi, please."

I continued to set the places but now Bambi's hands were stuffed in her pockets and she was staring at me. Realizing she wouldn't leave it alone, I leaned up against the wall and looked over at her. "I don't think it's going to work between me and Bradley."

"Why?" She frowned. "I thought we've been through this already."

"You know why, Bambi." I paused. "Between what he represents and me having an abortion, things haven't been the same."

"I don't like this for you two," she said. When she saw Bradley approaching, she leaned in and whispered. "Your marriage is the last stable one in this family. Don't let it go because of something that couldn't be avoided." Bambi walked away as Bradley approached me.

When she was gone he asked, "What was that about?" He looked in Bambi's direction. "She telling you to leave your husband?"

"Nothing, Bradley. Why you always tripping when it comes to Bambi? Who, by the way, is always on your side."

He rolled his eyes. "You and this secretive shit is driving me crazy."

"You acting like a guilty man," I said under my breath. "When the only thing I want to do is get this meeting over with. Tell me dear husband, do you have something to hide?"

"You disrespected me, Denim."

"What? How you sound?"

"You disrespected me when you had an abortion and that fucks me up. You listened to your mother over me and I gotta wonder who else you listening to."

After putting the last place setting down, he was about to walk back to the room to get dressed but I pulled his hand softly. "Bradley, how long are you going to be angry with me? I'm your wife. And no matter what we've gone through, I've always forgiven you. I'm asking for the same."

He snatched away and looked down at me. I saw his teeth gritting and knew he was trying to hold back. "You made a decision without me." He pointed in my face. "One that you knew would hurt. And I will never forgive you."

I could feel my stomach pull because I knew he was being honest. He was right. I made the decision to get rid of the baby but it was for the both of us. As wrong as my mother was, in a lot of ways, she was right. Neither Bradley nor me knew why Jasmine was born autistic. How could we be sure that it wouldn't happen again?

"Is there anything I can do to push us in the right direction?"

He took a deep breath and said, "You can start by getting your mother out of our house. Until that happens, I have nothing else to say to you." He stomped away.

Frustrated, I took a seat at the table and Race walked into the dining room and sat next to me. I could tell by the look in her eyes that something was wrong. "What's up?"

Race looked around her, leaned in and whispered, "Mellvue is still alive. Bambi been asking me if it's taken care of and I lied."

I put my hand over my head. Just seeing the look on Bambi's face a minute ago, I knew this would not be good. "Bambi just told me the chick was gone," I whispered. "She got plans to tell the bosses tonight and everything. You've got to tell her the truth."

"I can't."

"Race, this is not a good time to be holding back from Bambi. If she tells them a lie, it will ruin her credibility. I mean I thought you said that Roman was sick with the murder game."

"She is but something else is going on with her that she's not telling me about. I keep asking this chick if I can do something and every time she's like she's cool."

I frowned. "Well she took our money so she gotta do the job," I said point blank.

"I know," she sighed. "I just wish I knew what was up with her." She slammed her fist on the table. "Fuck!" she screamed out. "If Bambi asks you if the chick is alive can you lie for me?" she asked in a low voice. "I don't want her thinking I've been dropping the ball. I'm trying to get my own house and she talking about putting me out of the game because I'm slipping. You heard her the day Mellvue showed up."

"I got you," I said touching her hand. "But you gotta get over that shit with Carey. You killed her and now she's gone. Moping about it won't bring her back."

"I don't know if that's what's bothering me, Denim."

"Then what is it?"

"I'm not sure if I'm making the right decision about divorcing Ramirez."

"Then don't," I said excitedly. I wanted her to stay with him. "Give it some time. There's no rush."

"If only it was that easy." She sighed and got up.

"Where you 'bout to go?" I asked.

"To get dressed."

"Remember, we're wearing all black," I reminded her.

"I know."

"Where's Scarlett?" I asked.

"Get this shit. So Roman asked for her help awhile back. Today she called me and said she needed Scarlett on that favor. It has something to do with her having to lie about having a real job so she wanted Scarlett to pretend like she was her boss."

"Why Scarlett?" I frowned.

"Cause she's white," she laughed.

I shook my head and giggled too. "Old girl is wild," I responded. "I just hope after this shit is done, she takes lives like she's paid to do."

"If she don't then I'll have her taken care of."

"I already know," I laughed.

CHAPTER EIGHTEEN
BAMBI

Standing at the window, I grinned as I watched the black sedans pull up and park in the driveway outside of the bunker. I had to do a lot of shit to get the east coast bosses here and I wanted to be sure everything was perfect.

Excited, I closed the heavy burgundy curtain and faced my family. They were in their respective seats around the long cherry wood table. Dressed in all black, I was proud to say that they all exuded money. We hadn't looked this good in a long time. And I felt as if we were united.

We were Kennedys.

Scarlett's red hair hung over her shoulder and brushed against the straps of the black silk dress she wore. Denim's dreads were pulled in a neat ponytail and Race's brown hair was in a sharp bob that hung at her jawbone.

The fellas were looking lovely too. Camp in a pair of black jeans, black t-shirt and black jacket. Bradley in his two-piece suit with a designer button down shirt that he released the first three buttons on. Ramirez was sporting black velvet Tom Ford corduroys and a black shirt.

Although my brothers-in-law looked hot, Kevin's look was delicious. He was dipped in a double-breasted black suit with a red hanky stuffed in his jacket pocket. I wanted to fuck him and kill him at the same time and I knew his selections were on purpose.

They were meant to seduce me.

Good job, Mr. Kennedy.

By T. Styles

You succeeded.

"They're coming," I told my family as I walked slowly toward them. I stopped at the head of the table and stood next to Kevin. I caught the nigga looking at me. The long black dress that I wore with the slit down the side made way for my thigh every time I moved.

"I hope this works," Kevin said as he folded his arms over his chest. "You did a lot to get them here, Bambi. Hopefully shit won't backfire in our faces."

"Wake up, husband. It already has worked," I reminded him. "Now you should trust and support me."

"I'm here ain't I?"

Fuck Kevin!

Either he was jealous or holding onto animosity about our past beefs. Either way, I was in no mood for drama inside the camp tonight.

I turned my attention toward the door. When our trusted butler opened it, one by one the bosses trickled in. First inside was Nine Prophet of the infamous Prophet family. The collar of the black fur coat she was draped in stroked her high cheekbones and set off her gorgeous dark skin. My butler accepted her coat and I gently shook her tiny hand before shaking her husband's.

I heard that Nine's mother and father were brother and sister. And that her husband was actually her cousin. No matter what the circumstance, when it came to business she was deadly and didn't play.

She was one of Mitch's top customers and she commanded an army of almost a thousand men.

With her support alone, we were winning.

"Bambi, it's a pleasure to finally meet you," Nine said with a slight nod. It felt like I was in the presence of a queen and I knew that although young, no more than twenty years old if I'm guessing, she was a boss. She appeared regal and a slight smile rested on her face.

"The pleasure is all mine," I said softly. "The circumstances aren't the best but I'm glad you could make it."

"What better circumstance than war?" She winked.

"You have a beautiful home," her husband Leaf said politely. He handed me a bottle of Ace of Spades even though I requested that the guests bring nothing.

Classy.

"Thank you," I replied. "My sister will show you to your seats," I said as Denim approached.

The next bosses in line were Rasim and Snow Nami of the Nami family. This is business, I can't lie, but the moment that 6-foot something man hovered over me, he took my breath away. With tattoos all over his neck, I could see his muscles protruding through his black button down shirt.

His wife Snow was equally stunning. Much shorter than him, when I looked into her hazel brown eyes I could tell that she deserved to be at his side. I wondered how much a man as handsome as he was had put her through. "Thank you for inviting us," Snow said. "I've been looking forward to meeting you."

"The pleasure is all mine," I responded shaking her hand. "Thank you for coming."

After I shook Snow's hand, Rasim moved closer and I swallowed. "Whatever you need from us, we got you," Rasim said gazing at me a bit longer than necessary before walking inside.

"Thank you. That means a lot."

I don't know what made me do it but when I glanced behind me, Kevin wore a frown on his face.

Jealous ass nigga.

I'm sure he'd be trying to fuck me after this meeting was all said and done. Because although the men were attractive, I had no doubt that Nine Prophet with her body of a goddess and Snow with her elegant curves had his dick rock hard.

Female bosses were so intoxicating.

After greeting the Namis and the Prophets, the next group that trickled in was Carissa, Mercedes, Yvette and Lil C. Back in the day, they ran an operation called Emerald City. There was so much money coming out of Emerald City that their husbands were considered rock stars in Washington, D.C.

I'm not sure of the exact story but from what I'm told, although their men ran Emerald City, to expand their reach they put their girlfriends onto the city while they tended to business in their outside shops.

Shit was sweet and a lot of money was made until one of the men, who I believe fucked with Yvette, brought another bitch into the picture. This caused a feud amongst the men and compromised things. And like the saying bros before hoes, the women stayed together and moved their men out of Emerald City by taking command of their soldiers.

The last I heard, every last one of their men died.

Later, Lil C, Mercedes' son, ran Tyland Towers, which he called Camelot. He was doing pretty good too but eventually Emerald City and Tyland were torn down by a company called National Improvement for a Greater Generation Association, or NIGGA for short, and they lost everything.

This is where I came in.

Generally, I didn't fuck with new bitches but my good friend Toi introduced me to them after the tear down. Mercedes, Yvette and Carissa were down on their luck and I helped them out because she vouched for them.

I allowed them to stay in one of my homes and in return, they moved coke for me. Under my watch, before long, they reclaimed the new towers that the organization built and flooded them with our work. Not being able to battle the violence and keep the property drug free, NIGGA sold the property back to the government and now it belonged to Yvette and her crew.

Mercedes shook my hand and said, "Thanks for inviting us, Bambi." I never got over how beautiful she was. If I'm telling the truth, they were all stunning.

Mercedes' light skin was red probably because it was a bit chilly outside.

Carissa shook my hand next, her fine hair was pulled back into a ponytail and she looked as if she was part Indian.

Yvette greeted me last and her grip was firm. Although she was the shortest of the crew, I always got the impression that she was the most deadly, just like Race.

Unfortunately, I also sensed jealousy of my success whenever she was in my presence. A few times my instincts said to cut her off but Toi begged me not to. My friend was the only reason Yvette was still getting money and she was the only reason she was still alive.

Yvette smoothed her short haircut with her hand and looked at the bosses and then back at me. "I guess it's time for war."

"Indeed," I said as Denim showed them their seats.

With them out of the way, Lil C walked up to me next. A large gold medallion rested on his black t-shirt and the scent of his leather jacket was so strong I could tell it was new. He was young and a little arrogant but I could see he was born in the dope game and that made me respect him.

He reminded me of my sons, Melo and Noah.

He scratched his curly hair and smiled. "Looking good, Ms. Bambi," he said licking his lips. "Very good."

He was always coming on to me, which was hilarious in my book. This lil nigga couldn't handle one of my titties if I put the nipple on his lip. Let alone my pussy. The only reason I didn't hurt his feelings was because he was harmless. For now anyway. "Have a seat, C," I said shaking my head.

"My bad," he smiled raising his hands in the air.

The final person to walk in was Kelsi and I had great respect for him also. Just like Lil C, Kelsi was born in the dope game and used to move coke with his mother Janet.

Although he was from the D.C. area, he moved to Atlanta and made a huge name for himself. He exuded strength and when he stepped into my house there was something about him I respected immediately.

Although I knew he couldn't be any older than thirty, he still rocked a few grey hairs in his goatee.

Shaking my hand firmly, he handed me a bottle of Chateau Margaux, the most expensive wine in the world. Loving his swag, I gave it to the butler with a nod and he sat it on the table.

"Bambi Kennedy. It's a pleasure to finally meet you. Your reputation precedes you."

"Kelsi Stayley," I responded with a smile. "The pleasure is all mine." I gestured toward everyone else. I caught him checking out Denim and Bradley caught them looking at each other. "Please...have a seat."

With everyone now present, I swaggered over to the table. I was preparing to thank them for coming but Sarah walked in. She was wearing a white t-shirt and soiled grey sweatpants.

Leaning up against the wall, obviously drunk out of her mind, she said, "I'm sick of you bitches not inviting me to the party. With all these fine ass niggas in here." She eyeballed Kelsi, Rasim, Leaf and Lil C. "I'm a part of this family too, you know."

When I looked at Denim she appeared frozen.

Sarah raised her hand and that's when I saw the glass. Slithering her tongue into the cup, she lapped at the wine a little while looking at me through the bottom.

That was it!

I was done with this fat, ugly bitch.

I was headed over toward her to lay hands but Kevin got up and put his palm on my lower back. "I got her, baby." He kissed me on the cheek as if we were still a couple and for some reason, I was relieved.

As he ushered her hating ass from the place where only bosses roamed, I looked at the guests and said, "Sorry for the distraction. Let's eat and then do as bosses do."

Dinner was over and cocktails were served. "Where is Mitch?" Nine Prophet asked as she leaned

By T. Styles

back in the chair with her legs crossed. "Shouldn't he be present at this meeting?"

"He should, but considering that security is high, we feel it best to keep him out of it," Kevin responded.

"Besides, we're all grown," I joked. "We don't need daddy."

"So you don't trust us?" her husband responded.

"We're in the dope business," I replied, "where the motto is trust no one."

They all smiled.

"And yet you invite us to your home anyway," Nine winked at me.

"Trust is one thing," I said. "Respect is another. And you earned that."

Nine nodded and winked again. The chick had mad swag and I must admit I liked her a lot.

"Tell me something, what makes you think the Russians will try to take out our entire operation?" Kelsi questioned as he wiped his hand down his chin. "It seems a little ambitious."

"Because the hope is that if your operations are down, you won't have money to cop coke from Mitch," Denim said.

"And if you don't have money, Mitch isn't eating the same way he has in the past and his profits will be down," Bradley added. "So they're trying to smoke Mitch out to force him to do business with them."

"But if they can't get Mitch, why impact *our* businesses?" Yvette asked. "We don't buy from the Russians."

"Because eventually the Russians hope to bully you into a business relationship with them using whatever bullshit product they secure," Kevin responded.

"And we've gotten information that if you choose not to use their powder, once they've secured another connect, they will attack," I said.

"Any idea on how much this mothafucka wanna charge?" Kelsi asked.

"I'm not sure but I hear it's as high as forty percent," I said. "Way more than Mitch charges."

They moved around a little and I could see the agitation. "Why is all of this happening now?" Rasim asked. "The Russians haven't wanted in on our business before."

"They're doing this now because they want to deal directly with Mitch," Race replied. "And we won't let them."

"So why not let the niggas cop from Mitch straight up?" Lil C asked readjusting his gold chain on his chest. "Seems like all our problems would be eliminated with that."

"That's a good point," Snow responded. "We purchase directly from Mitch. So why can't they?"

Yvette frowned. "Oh, so ya'll get to go straight to Mitch?" she asked looking over at the Namis. "Because we gotta go through Bambi with a markup."

I could feel the tension in Yvette's voice and I didn't like it. "You deal through me because I brought you in when your other supplier dried up."

"Oh yeah, that's right," Scarlett said. "What was his name?"

"The nigga's name was Saint," Denim responded.

"Didn't he want to fuck you?" Scarlett continued. "And when you refused, he kidnapped you for three days before our men saved your life?"

Yvette rolled her eyes and sat back into her seat.

"Are you saying my prices aren't fair?" I asked returning to the subject now that my sisters put her in her place. "Because I know for a fact that I'm giving you a better deal than your first connect, Dreyfus. Who, by the way, was getting his product directly from Mitch."

"I'm not saying that your prices are unfair," she responded.

"Then what the fuck you saying then?" Denim snapped.

"Hold up, why you coming at my friend all hard and shit?" Carissa barked, slamming on the table with a closed fist. "She got a right to ask questions. Isn't that why we were all called? To weigh in on the matter?"

"Wasn't nobody even talking to you anyway," Mercedes said to Denim.

"Bitch, you sound crazy," Race said as she stood up. "This our mothafucking house! Check the Kennedy name on the door!"

"Sit down, bay," Ramirez said tugging on her elbow. She looked at him and took a seat. "I know it's a lot of tension in this room right now but we shouldn't be fighting each other." Ramirez looked at everyone and then his eyes rested on Yvette. "You don't have to use our coke if you don't want to, shawty. If you can get a better price, then so be it. The door is over there. Use your wings...they work." He pointed.

Yvette looked at Carissa, Mercedes and Lil C. I guess she didn't get the permission to walk out that she was looking for because she sat back in the chair, crossed her arms over her chest and stared at me. "I'm listening," she responded.

I liked Yvette. I really did but if she came at me sideways again I had intentions on snatching her heart out. But when I did, she wouldn't see it coming. It wouldn't be in a meeting with all of the bosses present, so that they would think that I couldn't control myself. It would be in private, within a dark alley.

Just her and I.

"Let's say the Russians do want war," Nine said bringing me back to the meeting at hand. "And let's say they try to dismantle our operations if we refuse to use their coke. What is your plan?"

"Yeah, why we here?" Kelsi asked.

"You're here because the Russians have connected with other bosses," I said. "Together they are calling themselves the Russian Cartel and they command a big army. I was hoping that we could do the same. Combine our soldiers and fight back. Together we are a legion."

"And where's Mitch again?" Rasim questioned.

"We have him held up for his protection," I responded. "Once we deal with the Russian Cartel then we'll let him go. But don't worry, while we have him in custody, business will still move as usual. Bricks are still being sold."

"And how does one deal with the Russian Cartel?" Snow asked.

"We kill them," I responded.

Silence.

Nine smiled and said, "War is a necessary evil."

I nodded. "Yes it is, friend."

"So when do you think they'll make a move?" Nine asked.

"One of their fiancés was murdered today," I said looking at Race. "The order was given by us in response to the men they killed in our organizations. We also took out their best soldier. A man by the name of Larry. And I'm sure because of it, they're angry and disabled." I paused. "I reason that they'll make another move on your camps any day now."

"Well if they do," Nine said with a smile on her face, "we will be ready."

"So are you all in?" I looked around the table. "Because I need an answer tonight. Can I see a show of hands?"

Starting with Nine Prophet, one by one, the bosses raised their hands. In my family, Race was the first followed by everyone else. And when I looked down at my husband he raised his hand too.

My pussy jumped.

I don't know why the small action caused my heart to pump rapidly but it did. Finally, he had my back.

"Thank you," I said to all of them, especially the nigga whose name I chose. "As you know, I invited you all to stay here in the bunker tonight and I hope that you will take me up on my offer. In the event the war is extra bloody, you and your families are welcome to come here for protection. This place is off the grid to everyone, including the police."

Nine stood up and Leaf went to grab her fur coat from the butler. "I appreciate the offer, friend, but my husband and I have a war to plan for in the privacy of our own home." She strolled over to me. She reminded me of Cleopatra. Strong, bold and elegant.

"Don't worry about us," Nine continued. "We will be ready for them." She extended her hand. "It is such a pleasure to be in the company of a real king. A real woman. I look forward to doing more business with you in the future."

I shook her delicate hand. "Same here."

I walked them to the door after they said their goodbyes to everyone. When they were gone I looked back at the table. "So is everyone else staying?"

They all nodded.

"I guess it's a celebration," Rasim said raising his wine glass in the air.

"The party before the storm," Lil C added.

I smiled and when I looked toward the back, I saw Sarah. She grinned at me and walked away.

I wondered how long she was standing there.

By T. Styles

CHAPTER NINETEEN
DENIM

Sitting by the fireplace, I was sipping a glass of wine after dinner when someone walked up behind me and said, "So how do you think this will all work out?"

When I turned around I was looking into Kelsi's handsome face. I shrugged. "I'm not sure but I think we will reign. But..."

"But what?" he asked refilling my glass with the expensive red wine I was drinking that he brought.

"But there will be a lot of blood."

He sighed and poured himself a glass before sitting the empty bottle on the ground. "From us or them?"

"From both organizations," I said.

He shook his head. "Spilled blood is never a problem unless it comes from your camp."

"I know. I just—"

My sentence was cut off when Bradley came from behind Kelsi and pushed him against the bricks next to the fireplace. Kelsi outstretched one hand, gripped Bradley's throat and squeezed. I tried to break them apart when Race, Scarlett, Kevin, Camp and Ramirez tapped Kelsi on the shoulder and pointed their weapons at Kelsi's head.

Kelsi released Bradley's throat and raised his hands in the air. "I was just defending myself. No harm done. No harm gained."

"That may be true but you need to leave," Bambi said firmly.

Kelsi walked slowly toward the door, confident and unmoved. He grabbed his jacket. Not one gun lowered. "If you're that insecure over your woman, maybe you don't deserve to have her."

Bradley made a move for Kelsi but Kevin stopped him. Kelsi laughed, shook his head and walked out of the door.

Chilling in my bedroom, I was smoking a blunt and looking at myself in the mirror. A second later, Bradley walked in. Everyone else was in the living room, sitting around the fireplace talking about the upcoming battle with the Russians and how Bradley played himself in front of Kelsi.

I was embarrassed.

I needed a break.

My marriage was not what I wanted it to be or what I knew it could be and I didn't understand why.

"Oh, I didn't know you were in here," he said. "I'll come back later. I wanted to take a nap."

Before he left, I said, "Baby," I stood up, "please don't leave. We need to talk because right now I'm confused."

"Confused about what?"

"Us. You. And the way you've been acting."

"I apologized to the nigga," he said waving it off. "Just like the rest of the bosses, he put the call in to have his available men meet at our other property to go over details." He paused. "He's not even tripping."

"That ain't the point, Bradley!"

He stood by the door with the knob in his grip. Looking down at the floor, he said, "What do you want from me, Denim? Me to change? Because I'm the same man I've always been. Maybe now you're just realizing it."

I shook my head because if that was true I was more horrified.

"Bradley, I've never, ever stepped out on you in our relationship. Or our marriage. But it seems like since you've been home, you don't realize that. All I want is for us to get back to us. Back to the way things were. Back to trusting and believing one another."

"We have a long way to go before things get back to normal, Denim."

"Can you at least tell me where to start?"

He sighed and released the door. "I told you what I needed to happen." He looked over at me. "For your mother to go."

Slowly I raised my head and looked into his eyes. "Okay," I said. "I'll tell her she has to bounce. If that will let you know how much I love you, it's done."

He strolled over to me. When he reached me he stared down and said, "Are you serious?"

"Yes, Bradley," I said standing up before walking away. "I'll arrange for her to rent a new place until hers is finished. Just give me a few days and she'll be gone. That's all I ask. "

"Thank you, baby." He kissed my lips. "You don't know how much this means to me."

"Bradley, did something happen to you in jail? That you don't want to tell me?"

He separated from me and walked toward the door. "Just focus on your mother, Denim. Everything else will work itself out."

CHAPTER TWENTY
RACE

I was sitting at the fireplace with Bambi and she was giving me a cold stare. It seemed like ever since Bradley laid hands on Kelsi, shit had gotten out of control. The only good part was that each boss present gave us ten percent of their available soldiers.

Now I had to clear the air with Bambi.

"I have to tell you something," I whispered. "Because I hate keeping secrets from you. But I'm afraid that you will judge me."

She looked at me and wiped her hand down her face. "Mellvue is still alive?" she asked.

Instead of going with the out she gave me, I got scared. "No," I said clearing my throat. "I told you I took care of it."

"Race," she said through clenched teeth. "Why are you lying to me? I haven't heard one thing about her murder. How come?"

"I don't know, Bambi."

"Do you realize how you'll make me look if this bitch is still breathing? The least you can do is be honest."

Before I could answer her, my phone rang. I pulled it out of my purse and saw it was Sarge. Without responding to Bambi, I said, "Do you see Roman?"

"I have her in my sights."

Through clenched teeth, I said, "Keep her there. I'm about to call her cell phone right now." I hung up with Sarge and dialed Roman's number. This bitch played too many games and now I wanted her gone.

By T. Styles

Besides, I boasted heavily about this chick to the family only for her to be unworthy of my attention. Maybe I needed to step out of the family business after all.

But who was I if I wasn't in this game?

Her phone rang twice before she answered. "Yes, Race."

"Why is she still alive?" I asked getting straight to the point.

"Because I—"

"I think you've allowed my kindness to give you the wrong impression about me," I said cutting her off. "About who I really am. So let me be clear. I am the most dangerous woman you know."

I could hear her heavy breathing as if she was irritated but I didn't give a fuck. Something was up with this chick and I was tired of trying to figure out what.

I could feel Denim, Scarlett and Bambi looking at me so I stepped further away from everyone to keep my conversation private.

"You want that bitch dead?" Roman yelled through the phone.

"I want you to do your fucking job!"

"Is that what you *really* want?" she said getting louder.

I could hear the car revving up but I didn't know what she was doing.

"Then I'll give you what you asking for!" Roman continued.

"What are you about to do?" I asked. "Roman!"

Although she wasn't answering, I could hear her driving in the background so I stayed on the line. Suddenly the car was cut off and I heard her open the door. Not even a minute later, I heard screaming followed by a gun firing four times.

I knew what she was doing without her even telling me.

She killed Mellvue in broad daylight.

I was trembling. This bitch lost her mind. "Bambi, let me use your cell right quick," I said walking over to her. With one phone still on my ear, I dialed Sarge's number on Bambi's line and pressed it to my other ear. "Did she do what I think she did?" I asked him.

"Yeah."

"Did anybody see her?"

"Everybody there saw her. The chick was outside having a barbeque when your girl walked up on her and killed her in the open. Not sure why Mellvue was on the grill since it's cold as shit out here but she was."

I sighed. "Bring Roman to me." I hung up on him and handed Bambi back her phone. Bambi's forehead was wrinkled and she was glaring at me. I knew I couldn't lie to her anymore.

Patiently but angrily, I waited on Roman to return to the cell phone. When she did, Roman asked me, "Satisfied?"

Breathing heavily, I calmly said, "Meet me. Now."

"I got shit to do. I can't do it today."

"That's not an invitation. Look in your rearview mirror." I paused for a while so that she could see the trail of Hummers I knew were following her. I figured Sarge pulled up next to her car because I could hear the Temptations CD he always played in the background.

"Follow him, Roman," I said. "He'll bring you to me."

I stood in front of Roman as she sat in a chair inside of one of our buildings. Sarge and five other men stood behind me and they waited for my word. "Before I kill you, I need you to tell me what the fuck were you thinking today," I said calmly. "I'm a good judge of character but I must admit, I didn't see your unprofessionalism coming. First time for everything."

Instead of answering the question, Roman focused on the army of men behind me. "Let me ask you something. If you have all of them, why did you want my services? It's obvious anybody could've done the job."

"I don't answer your fucking questions!" I yelled stepping closer to her. I looked back at Sarge because I was done with this chick. She'd humiliated me for far too long. "Kill this bitch. I'm done with her."

They were about to put her out of her misery until Roman yelled, "My son was kidnapped. And now he's...now he's dead!"

Upon hearing Roman's words, I raised my hand, stopping the bullets seconds before they zipped through the air and toward her body. Turning around, I strolled back up to her and asked, "Who kidnapped your son?"

"Her name is Yoko Lighthouse."

"You mean that little bitch?" I asked raising my hand like I was measuring an invisible child's height. I knew of the woman but she was not any real threat. At least I didn't think so. "Who lives in Magnolia Gardens apartments?"

"Yes." She paused. "She wanted me to kill some people. Some witnesses involved in a case against her brother. When I refused, she took my son and then...and then killed him."

For the first time, she broke down in front of me. She was so tough that I never knew she could be hit emotionally.

Sarge and the other soldiers exhaled. I guess everything now made sense to all of us. Sarge liked the hotheaded killer as much as I did but neither of us understood her recent moves until now.

"You should've come to me earlier, Roman," I said. Killing a child was already bad but killing a child on purpose drove me up a wall. "I could've helped you!"

"I wanted to do it on my own," she said as tears rolled down her face. "I was afraid that the more people were involved, the harder it would be to get him back. And I rejected your friendship in the process. I'm sorry." She shook her head. "I just wanted my baby."

"Are you sure he's dead?" I asked calmly.

"Yes...I mean no. Yoko said he was dead but I haven't seen his body yet."

I exhaled. "Carey trusted you. So I will too." I paused. "What do you need?"

"I want my son back, so that I can bury him." She looked at my men. "But if I can't...if I can't, I want Yoko's life. And then I want out of this contract."

The next day Bambi was standing in front of me and I was sitting at the dining room table. "Do you

By T. Styles

realize how stupid you made me look?" Bambi asked. "I told them that Mellvue was dead and she wasn't. What were you thinking?"

"I wanted things to go smoothly. I wanted you to know that I could handle things because you were talking about cutting me off. Something I couldn't stand!"

"Ain't no need in getting mad at her," Denim said. "What's done is done. Now the question is, what are we going to do about it?"

Bambi looked at me but I could tell I ruined the trust. "Are you sure this bitch is dead now?" she asked me.

"It's all over the news, Bam," Denim said. "Saw it this morning."

Bambi seemed relieved but I could tell I was not her favorite person anymore. "Set a meeting up with Roman. I'll speak to her."

We were back at the location where I first introduced Bambi to Roman. And Bambi didn't waste any time getting right into it. "I'm disappointed in you, Roman," Bambi said softly. "And it isn't for the reason you think."

"Then what is it for?" Roman asked through clenched teeth.

"I'm disappointed that you didn't come to us from the onset. When you first needed help. We could've ended this a long time ago."

"I didn't want to get you involved. But now I need to be there for my family. My husband doesn't know that our son has been murdered and I have to go home and explain everything to him. All I want is to get out of the contract after I find Yoko."

"I'm sorry, Roman. I really am. But I can't let you out of the agreement. Over the past couple of weeks, you have proven to be invaluable to my organization. And even after your mishap today with Mellvue, for some reason you were able to complete the job without people recognizing you. You're an enigma. And I'm at war with the Russians." She paused. "I need the best on my team. I need you."

Roman held her head down and I felt sorry for her. I knew what it meant to want out but not be able to leave. It was something like my marriage. But Bambi was right; this was business. "But it's not in my heart anymore," Roman said. "To kill, I mean."

Bambi laughed hysterically. "Of course it's in your heart, my dear. Once a killer, always a killer. Use the anger and continue to be the best. In the end, for people like you and me, anger and murder are all we have." With a lowered brow, Bambi said, "Live with it or die."

The weirdest shit happened. After Roman and Bambi met, Roman's son Sailor was returned to her. The little dude was actually alive. But to make sure that our new killer would be freed up, we decided to take out her enemy.

It was eerily silent at the place where Yoko lived for the moment. The right side of the street was lined with eight of our Hummer trucks with green matte paint jobs. Three of our soldiers stood in front of each with the exception of the Hummer directly across from where Yoko, Roman's enemy, would stand.

Me, my sisters and Roman all stood in front of the vehicle closest to Yoko's hideout. When the midget came outside Bambi stepped forward. She wore green fatigues and her long flowing brown hair blew in the wind. Roman was leaning on the truck, shrouded in a black hoodie with white paint over her face and black paint over her eyes.

This bitch was thorough and I was so glad she was on our team.

Yoko looked scared as she stared at all of us. "So this is how I die?" Yoko yelled to Roman who remained leaning on the truck. "Your son is safe, Roman," she yelled. "I didn't kill him even though I told you I did. I would've never hurt him." She rubbed her growing belly. "I'm pregnant too, you know."

Silence.

Although Yoko made it seem like she returned him, from what I was told, the little boy fought his way out of his captor's possession and an old lady returned him to his family.

She didn't give up anything.

"When we were younger you had a code," Yoko continued. "To never kill the innocents." She swallowed. "Will you keep my baby alive? Do you still honor that code?"

Roman chuckled. "You right, Yoko. When we were younger, I did operate by a code. But you taught me that having a code was dumb. Do you remember what you said?"

"N...no," she stuttered.

"Well I do. You told me to leave the code shit to computer programmers. And I told you that one day you'd want someone to have a code." She paused. "Well I guess that day has arrived."

"Roman, please, I'm begging you."

"I know you're hurting, Yoko. I cried too. I lost the only people I cared about because of you. So tell me something. What the fuck I look like caring about that demon growing in your belly now?"

Silence.

"You ready?" Bambi asked Roman.

"Yes."

"Give the word and the men will act."

The soldiers cocked their weapons and aimed at Yoko, ready for Roman's word.

"Wait a minute," Roman said raising her hand.

I thought she had a change of heart. Instead, she walked slowly across the street. It was so silent you could hear the leaves rustle on the trees. Roman's hands were stuffed in her pockets and when she was finally upon Yoko, she looked down at her.

Without a word, Roman removed a switchblade from each pocket and plunged them into the sides of her neck. Blood spurted out of Yoko's flesh and Roman mouthed, "Goon."

I knew in that moment we had a secret weapon. She would be used to save our operation and get closer to the Russians. It was definitely time to battle.

CHAPTER TWENTY-ONE
THE RUSSIANS

*A*rkadi was pacing next to a table inside of an old abandoned IHOP restaurant. He was distraught and incensed with anger. They met there whenever they couldn't get to their hideout in D.C. Right now they were in Baltimore, Maryland, not too far from Jersey, D.C. and Virginia.

Inside of the restaurant were fifteen Reapers waiting for leadership.

"They killed my fiancé," he yelled at Iakov as if he were unaware. "And all you want to talk about is money and profit margins! What about her, brother?" He paused. "She was only woman I ever loved!" Each time he yelled, his face reddened as sweat dripped down his cheeks. "I want my revenge and I won't stop until I have it!"

Iakov slowly walked toward Arkadi. Standing over him, he placed one hand on his shoulder and used his other one to slap him. "You better get your life together and look around you." He stepped out of his way so that he could see that fifteen of the Reapers were around the table waiting on action. "You need level head. Never show weakness in front of warriors. You'll lose their respect forever."

Arkadi wiped the sweat off his face and backed up. "But I want revenge, brother," he whispered.

"Then get the revenge you seek." He paused. "Lead them to destruction."

Arkadi gazed up at his brother and wiped the sadness from his face. Slowly he swaggered toward the table and placed both hands on top of it. Staring at the *young men before him, he said, "I want you to bring me their—"*

His message ended abruptly when a hail of bullets came crashing into the restaurant. As they ripped through the foundation of the building, it seemed as if there wasn't a safe place in sight.

When Iakov saw a few of the men take bullets to the upper body he rushed up to his brother and knocked him to the floor. Together the both of them crawled toward the back of the restaurant to protect their lives.

Gunfire continued to tear into the walls and when it stopped, the Russians remained lying down until fifteen minutes passed and the smell of gunpowder filled the air.

Slowly both men stood up and walked toward the table. The scene was gruesome. Blood and guts covered everything in sight. The assassins successfully killed all but two, the most dangerous two.

The Russians.

"Who do you think it was?" Arkadi asked.

"Don't be stupid, brother," Iakov responded.

"But how did the Kennedys know where we held meetings?"

"The same way Mellvue found them." Iakov walked around the table, taking in all of its gore. "They researched using reputable resources. I won't stop until every last one of those chorn is dead! I don't care if it's the last thing I do."

CHAPTER TWENTY-TWO
SCARLETT

Sitting at the dining room table with a vegetable omelet in front of me, I was slowly settling into depression. Another sat across from me on a beautiful cream plate with red strawberries around the perimeter. I prepared breakfast for two because I thought Camp would join me.

But after the meal was finished, he came downstairs in a hurry to break our meeting off. "I'm sorry, baby. But I have an important meeting with Swanson. I'll have to take a rain check."

"Can I go with you?"

He ran his hand from the front to the back of my hair before kissing me on the forehead. "Not this time, baby. He wants to meet with me alone." Ever since he left, I wondered what they were talking about. Would Swanson tell him all of my secrets?

Without giving me a chance to be submissive to his will?

I was about to scrape both plates off into the trashcan when Ramirez came downstairs. His slippers scraped against the hardwood floor. "Oh, hey, Scarlett," he yawned before scratching his belly. He wasn't wearing a shirt, just grey pajama pants, and his muscles seemed to buckle as he moved. "Where's everybody?"

"They went to take care of some business," I sighed. "You know the saying. You're not a Kennedy unless you have something else to do."

He chuckled. "Tell me about it."

"So why aren't you gone?"

"Kevin told me he had everything under control. From what I'm told, the hit on the Russians was successful. So now it's just a waiting game."

I nodded. "Whose is this?" he asked pointing at the omelet.

"It was for Camp, but you can have it if you want."

He quickly sat down and pulled the plate toward him. "Hell yeah I want this bitch. I thought I was going to have to eat some cereal. Good looking out." He chuckled picking up the fork and stabbing into the omelet. "I can't remember the last time I got a home cooked meal." He swallowed and smiled. "Damn, girl. What you put in this?"

I grinned, pleased he enjoyed it. "Seafood, cheese, green peppers. Stuff like that."

"Well you did a good damn job."

Remembering what he just said, I asked, "So you haven't had a good meal from Race lately?"

He stuck a piece of food in his mouth, chewed for a few seconds and put the fork down. It clanked on the table. "I know you know the status of our situation."

"I wasn't trying to be nosey, Ramirez. I'm sorry."

"I know, ma," he responded. "I'm used to dealing with the fact that we may be over. I mean, what can you do when the person you love doesn't want you anymore? It's just tough hearing it."

I laughed. "You're asking me? The woman who is married to your brother who wants a divorce? And is only staying around until we find Master?"

"I'm sorry, Scarlett. I didn't mean to be insensitive." He paused. "How you holding up with Master missing?"

I swallowed and tried to pretend as if I didn't know where my son was. "I'm trying to make it.

Things would be easier if I knew Camp would be with me no matter what."

"You're doing better than me. I don't know how to deal with this shit, Scarlett." He shook his head. "I love Race. I just want her to love me back." He paused. "I feel like no matter what I do or say, she'll never be able to see that. And the shit hurts. I've fucked many. I've had more orgies than I can remember. But I've never loved another woman before Race."

I placed my elbows on the table and rested my face in my hands. "I don't know if we can do anything about being rejected but deal with it." I put my hands down. "Every day I pray that an idea comes to me. Every day I pray that Camp will see me for the woman I could be if he would just give me a chance. But nothing I say or do seems to work. He hates me."

"He doesn't hate you."

"That's what it feels like, Ramirez." Tears rolled down my face. "I wish I could take back every foul thing I did to him so that he would give me another chance at our marriage."

"I feel the same way. Had I known bringing Carey into the picture would've compromised my shit, I would've never done it. But now it's too late." He sighed. "I guess we both have to deal with the fact that things may be finished in our marriages."

Although what he was saying was true, I didn't want to hear it. Suddenly I cried so deeply I couldn't control myself. Ramirez pushed the chair back and ran over to me. Lifting me into his arms, I rested my face in the pit of his chest.

He smelled good.

Something like coconut and baked apples.

For some reason, I felt myself heating up and when I looked up at him, he was looking directly at me. Like I belonged to him.

Unhurriedly he lowered his head and kissed me softly on my lips. Electric jolts coursed through my body. Things were moving so fast and I couldn't stop them if I tried. In a matter of seconds, he turned me around and my hands were pressed against the cool table. Thinking he was about to do the ultimate, push inside of me, I was sweetly surprised when he kissed me on the neck instead.

"I know this is wrong," he said as he ran his tongue along the side of my neck and up toward my ear. "But I need you right now, Scarlett." His breath was heavy and heated up my lobe. "Can I make love to you? If you don't want me, all you have to say is no."

"Yessssss."

Without delay, he eased into me.

"Fuck," he moaned. "Judging by how wet you are, I can tell that you need me too."

He was right. I hadn't been with a man since Ngozi. Camp refused to sleep with me or like he said, "Give me the wrong idea." Although it felt good, I knew the guilt about what I was doing would stay with me forever.

But for now, I would enjoy every second of this moment.

Sitting in my car, I was trying to figure out where to go. I was ashamed I fucked my brother-in-law and ashamed to have betrayed Race. All of my life I seemed to allow my feelings to lead me.

I was lonely.

I was confused and I was scared.

Knowing that I may have destroyed a marriage beyond repair caused me to hate myself. Should I tell her? Or keep the secret moment that Ramirez and I shared private?

I was clutching the steering wheel, trying to figure out what to do when my phone rang. It was Swanson. "I just met with your husband."

My heart thumped wildly. "And what did you tell him?"

"I told him that I might have some very important information."

"And what is that?"

"Come now, Scarlett. Don't play coy. You know exactly what I'll tell him. Unless I can be convinced otherwise."

I leaned back in the seat and put my hand on my head. My pussy was still moist from my indiscretions with Ramirez. I just wanted all of this to end. To go away.

And suddenly running away from everything sounded like a good idea. I had enough money to bounce and I decided that would be my plan. But first I would meet with him.

"What do you want, Swanson?"

He exhaled and said, "I'm going to text you an address. When you get there you'll see a black sedan behind the building. I'll be inside of that vehicle with my dick in my hand. You're a smart girl. You'll know what to do from there."

When I arrived at the address, I spotted the car right away. I could hear soft jazz music playing from the car and my stomach flipped. Slowly I approached the vehicle and he unlocked the door. I slid inside and he adjusted the volume of the music, making it lower. I looked over at him and for a second he refused to say a word.

"So how does it feel to fuck a nigger every night?" he asked. "To be married to one? Do you feel dirty?"

My jaw dropped because I couldn't believe what he was saying. "You tell me, Swanson. Aren't you fucking one yourself?"

He laughed. "It's different for a white man. We own everything about the black race, including their women. But to sleep with a nigger and have his children as a white woman is unacceptable."

I could feel my forehead tightening.

"Tell me, my beautiful redhead," he continued, "is the rumor true? About them having big dicks?"

I was getting frustrated and angry at the same time. "I'm here, Swanson. Now what do you want from me to keep my secrets safe?"

"Why would you give your son up?" He positioned himself so that he was looking directly into my eyes. "It's obvious how much Camp loves him. Why give him away when his father wants to be in his life? I'm curious."

I looked down at my shaky hands. "I did what I thought I had to do at the time."

He unzipped his pants and released his dick. Stroking it to a thickness, he said, "Fuck all of that. Get over here and top me off." He paused. "And I don't want none of that lazy licking shit either. I want you to suck it just like you do for that nigger, redhead. How do the blacks say? Let me see what that mouth do!"

When I saw his little limp stick I tried to determine how I was going to prevent myself from throwing up. Slowly I eased toward him. I guess I was moving too slowly because he grabbed the back of my head and pushed my face down against his penis. It rubbed against my cheekbone and smelled like rubber. Like he was wearing a condom and took it off earlier.

Did he just have sex with someone else and now he was using me?

I was just about to open my mouth when the window on his side came crashing in. Shards of glass sprinkled against the top of my head and in his groin. When I looked up, I was staring into the green eyes of Roman.

"Duck," she said before pressing the gun to his head and blowing his brains out.

Although I could feel his limp body press against me, I didn't raise my head immediately. I wanted to be sure it was over.

Then I heard Roman whisper, "Goon."

That was all the assurance I needed.

When Swanson called earlier and told me to meet him, I decided to contact Roman and ask her to return the favor I did for her. She didn't let me down and the moment I saw his bloody head busted open, I felt relieved.

Quickly I got out of the car and walked toward her. She was with another guy who was pulling Swanson's bloody body out of the car and to the ground.

"Who's he?" I asked referring to her partner.

"My right hand," she said. "Don't worry. He's safe."

I looked over at her partner and back at her. I wasn't in any position not to believe her. So far, she'd proven to be trustworthy. "I heard your son is back home," I said to her.

She grinned. "Yes and I'm so grateful. I thought my boy was dead and he was alive."

I smiled. "Thank you for this." I paused looking down at Swanson's corpse. "I don't have to stress to you how important it is that you keep my privacy."

"I didn't get this far in the business by not being able to hold water. Your secret is safe with me, Scarlett. Now go, I have it from here."

When I got home I walked straight to the laundry room and removed my bloody blouse. I grabbed one of Camp's "Find Master" t-shirts and slogged toward my room. When I got there Camp was sitting on the edge of the bed waiting on me.

The moment I saw his face, I was shook. His eyebrows were tight and he was glaring at me. Did Ramirez tell him that we fucked? Without even giving me a heads up.

"Are you okay?" I asked with a half-smile on my face. Guilt all over my body. I tossed my purse on the dresser.

He looked at it and said, "Why you got blood on your bag?"

I looked at my purse and screamed inside. I did such a good job of covering my tracks and I still left a clue. "I think that's ketchup," I lied.

"Where were you, Scarlett?" he asked standing up.

I backed up into the wall. "What are you talking about?"

"I asked where the fuck were you?" he screamed pointing at the floor.

Judging by his actions, I could tell that he knew about me and Ramirez.

I was sure of it.

"Baby, I had to make a few runs," I lied. "To get my toes done and shit like that. Why?"

"I know about my son, Scarlett. I know everything." Tears rolled down his face and he was trembling. "How could you stand by and watch me struggle when you know how much I love my boy? What type shit is that?"

"Baby, what are you talking—"

He yanked a fist full of my hair and pulled me down to my knees. "Bitch, don't lie to me!" he screamed as if I weren't his wife. "I fucking know! I know everything!"

He released my hair and I scooted away from him. My back pressed against the wall and I brought my knees to my chest. I was crying but my voice felt caught in my throat.

"I will never forgive you for this shit." He grabbed his keys and wallet off the dresser. "Swanson is setting things up to go get my son after he handles whatever he has to later."

I figured Swanson was talking about fucking me. The thing was, he was dead now.

"But when I get my kid, I'm going to hold a meeting with my family," Camp continued. "And in that meeting I will make sure that everyone knows I want you out of here."

"But where will I go?" I sobbed. "I don't have anyone but you."

"That's not my problem anymore!"

CAMP

Camp was driving his silver Aston Martin and thinking about his life. Tears rolled down his face because he knew his marriage was officially over. His wife was sicker than he ever imagined and he couldn't see sharing his bed or his life with her. His only priority was his son and he didn't care what anyone thought about how he would handle his marriage.

"Who are you really, Scarlett?" he said to himself as he continued to drive down the street. He was trying to understand why he didn't realize how sick Scarlett really was.

Thinking about his son, he picked up his cell phone and called Swanson. When he got his voicemail, he left a message. "I know you out handling business now. But when you return I want to take you up on the offer to read Scarlett's file. I didn't want to know about her past before but I changed my mind. Hit me when you can."

When he arrived at the light, he punched his steering wheel in anger. He knew his family wouldn't take his dismissal of Scarlett well but he hoped they'd stand by his side, especially when they learned what she did with Master.

He lowered his head for one second when suddenly it felt like time stopped. A hail of bullets rained from all directions into the car. He tried to reach for his weapon in the glove compartment but he was unsuccessful.

He already took bullets in his shoulder and thigh and was doing his best to slide into the backseat. But he only made it halfway when the rest of the Reapers gang moved in closer to the vehicle and emptied their automatic weapons into the car.

When they were done, Camp lay lifeless.

CHAPTER TWENTY-THREE
DENIM

What the fuck is going on?
Standing in the middle of the madness, I couldn't believe what Bambi just told me. Over and over I replayed her words in my mind hoping I heard them incorrectly.

Camp was dead.

I remembered the dream that I had a while back, the one with a coffin being dropped in the ground with the Kennedy name on top of it. And yet I felt like the bloodshed was far from over.

Bambi said there would be loss but I never thought it would happen like this.

Scarlett was sitting on the sofa, her face beet red. Bambi sat on her left and Race on her right as they both tried to console her. But how do you console a woman who has lost her husband? I didn't know about Scarlett but there'd be nothing anybody could tell me, not even Jesus Christ himself, if something happened to Bradley.

When I looked over at my brothers-in-law, I never saw them so distraught. Kevin was leaning against the wall. His head pointed up towards the ceiling and one hand covered his face.

Ramirez was sitting at the table with Bradley. A bottle of liquor sat between them and they were drinking glass after glass.

I couldn't believe what we'd gotten ourselves into. What started with us wanting to defend our operation ended in us losing a member of our family.

Still, something had to be done. We couldn't lie around and take this shit. If ever there was a time to strike back, now was it.

I walked into the middle of the living room and looked at everyone. "What are we going to do now?" I asked.

I guess my voice was too low because they didn't respond or seem to hear me. So I spoke louder. I wanted to be heard over the crying. Over the, *'I can't believe he's gone'* outbursts. Someone took a shot at our family and we had to fire back. "What the fuck are we going to do about this disrespect?" I screamed.

Now I had their attention.

I took a deep breath and said, "I know this shit hurts. And I know we're going to feel this forever. I lost a brother-in-law who I loved." I looked at the fellas. "You lost a brother and Scarlett a husband. But them mothafuckas need to be dealt with tonight." I pointed at the floor. "I say we do what needs to be done before they take somebody else from us. When the war is over, we can cry then."

"She's right," my mother said walking up behind me.

The moment I heard her voice, the hairs on my skin stood up. I knew she was about to say something reckless and I was horrified at what might happen to her.

"What ya'll need to do is get the fuck up and find them niggas who shot that boy," she said sitting at the table with Bradley and Ramirez. She poured herself some liquor in Bradley's cup and downed it before slamming it back on the table. "I thought ya'll were gangsters. None of you seemed to have a problem pointing a gun at me but now look at you." She poured another cup and downed that too. "When someone kills one of your own, you're sitting around crying. Look like some wangsters to me."

I walked over to her, leaned down and whispered in her ear, "Mama, now is not the time for this shit. I'm warning you."

"Why ain't it? They sitting around acting like the rest of ya'll ain't alive. Shit, if it was me I would—"

"You would do what?" Bradley asked cutting her off. He was standing over top of her with clenched fists and I wondered if this time he would use them.

And if I would care.

"Get the fuck from around me, boy," she said. "I'm just speaking my opinion like everybody else 'round here. I'm tired of ya'll leaving Mitch and me in the room like we in a refugee camp. We both getting sick of it. It's time you learn to respect me."

Upon hearing Mitch's name, Bambi stood up and walked toward her. The anger was written all over her face. "You've been consorting with Mitch?" she asked calmly.

"Not sure what consorting is but yes, we had a conversation or two." She paused. "Why? What's the problem? I'm a grown woman and he's a grown man."

Bambi stared at my mother with hatred. I'd seen that look one other time. When she was beefing with Aunt Bunny and now Bunny was dead.

My mother could be messy but I didn't like how Bambi was looking at her. After all, she was still my mother. "You okay, Bam?" I asked.

Bambi's gaze turned toward me. She leaned in and said, "Get rid of her, Denim. I'm feeling violent and the last thing I want to do is react on your mother. But if she stays a minute longer, I will attack." She walked over to Kevin and he stared down at her for a second before pulling her into an embrace. I hadn't seen them express love to one another like that in months.

I turned toward my mother. "Come, on, ma," I said softly.

"Why I always got to go? For once in a conversation, why can't someone else leave?"

"Now is not the fucking time!" I yelled. "Now come the fuck on!" I grabbed her by her arm and walked her toward her room.

I turned around momentarily and looked at Bambi. Her face rested against Kevin's chest and she was staring directly at my mother.

I knew even more that I had to get her out of there. Or else, like Bunny, she may not survive.

CHAPTER TWENTY-FOUR
THE RUSSIANS

*A*rkadi sat in a corner as he watched Iakov, Derrick, Jim and Vito pour champagne in their mouths from the bottle, each celebrating their recent victory.

Camp Kennedy's murder.

They were finally able to do something none of them thought was possible...kill a King.

Although they were memorializing their successes inside of their hideout, Arkadi was still bitter. He lost his fiancé and no matter how hard he tried, he simply couldn't move past it. To relieve his pain, he started hitting the bottle harder but lately he moved to something a little stronger...powder cocaine.

As his thoughts swirled, he fixated his stare on his brother. Despite Camp being killed, Arkadi felt that his brother undermined him by not wanting to fight harder to avenge Mellvue's death. What was one Kennedy dead when there were plenty more alive? He started to believe that Iakov felt as if he were in charge of the Russian Cartel when it was both of their operation.

After laughing it up with the other bosses, Iakov grabbed a half-full bottle of champagne from the ice bucket. He also scooped up two flutes and walked over to Arkadi. Trails of water droplets splashed against the hardwood floor with each step.

"Why are you sitting over here alone, brother?" Iakov yelled in an inebriated state. "Be joyful! After so much time we are realizing what we always knew. That we are the real kings." He poured champagne in both glasses and gave Arkadi one.

"What makes you think I'm not pleased? Because I don't laugh it up with a Dago and two niggers?" He gulped all of his champagne and tossed the flute on the floor. It crashed against it, thereby giving him unwanted attention from the bosses.

Realizing his brother was in a worse position than he imagined, Iakov drank the champagne, sat the bottle and glass down and looked at him. "I haven't forgotten about your woman."

Arkadi laughed. "I wish I could believe you."

"It is true. And I'll show you better than I can tell you." He placed his hand on his shoulder. "Wait until you see what I have in store for you next. If this doesn't avenge your woman, I don't know what will."

CHAPTER TWENTY-FIVE
BAMBI

My husband was sitting on the edge of the bed with his head lowered. I knew we had to make moves after Camp's death but he was in pieces from losing his brother.

I wasn't sure if he was capable of an attack.

I wanted to say something that I thought would help get him through this moment. Something to give him strength now.

"I'm sorry," I whispered.

He looked up at me, his eyes red and swollen. "This isn't your fault, Bambi. I don't want you thinking that shit."

"That's not what I mean," I said softly. "I'm sorry for what I did to your aunt Bunny. I'm sorry for taking the one person you cared about outside of me and the kids and your brothers." I paused. "I don't know if it's possible but I'm hoping in the future that you will be able to forgive me. And if not, I'm willing to die trying."

His expression went from sorrow to something I couldn't read. He stood up and walked toward me. I guess I picked the wrong thing to say because I felt like he was about to hurt me. Instead, he pulled me to his body and my face nestled into the center of his chest.

"You never said sorry, until now," he exhaled. "That's all I ever wanted, Bambi. I thought you didn't care about how I felt. I thought I didn't matter." He kissed me on my forehead and my cheeks before moving to my lips. "Thank you, baby. You'll never know how much your apology means to me." And then he looked into my eyes, his lips quivering. "I...I forgive you now."

And just like that, I could feel the tension that stood between us for so long disappear. It was as if all of the months we barely said two words to each other didn't happen. As if he never left my side. My husband returned to me during his darkest hour and I was eternally grateful.

When he left almost two years ago, I took care of this family on my own. I was in charge of keeping my sisters moving forward even when I didn't have the strength. When he came back I thought I didn't need him.

I was wrong.

I was stronger with my husband, not apart from him and I would never allow time to pass between us again. Losing Camp reminded me that time was too precious to waste on bullshit.

I was a Kennedy.

And he was the man who chose me.

He placed both hands on the sides of my face and looked down at me. "We have to stick together. Shit is about to get thick and I can't take something happening to you."

Suddenly there was a frantic knock at the door. When it opened, it was Race. "You gotta come to the living room. Melo and Noah are fist fighting!"

When I walked into the living room only to see my sons brawling all over the floor, I thought I was seeing things. Noah was on top of Melo, pulling at the blue t-shirt he was wearing until he pulled the collar out of place. Because they were identical, he looked as if he were trying to kill himself.

Why were they fighting?

I was stuck, unable to make a move. Luckily, Kevin rushed past me and grabbed Noah's white t-shirt before he came down on his brother's face with a beer bottle.

Finally able to move, I quickly grabbed Melo.

"What the fuck is going on in here, sons?" Kevin yelled as he pushed Noah back so that he could not engage Melo again.

At this point, the entire family assembled in the living room.

"It's nothing, dad," Melo said as he paced the floor with his hands over his face. Sweat poured down his forehead and I saw the veins on his temple throb.

"Don't tell me it's nothing!" Kevin yelled. "I got eyes and what I see right now is my sons fighting each other! As if we didn't just find out your uncle was murdered. As if we don't have enough pain in this family already." He paused. "Now what the fuck is going on?"

Melo held his head down and shook it. "He disrespected mama," he said trying to catch his breath. He leaned up against the wall. "And I stole him in the face for it."

I looked at Noah, trying to figure out what was going on.

"Is this true?" Kevin asked.

Silence.

"Son, answer me," Kevin yelled at Noah. "Why are you disrespecting your mother?"

Noah looked at me with rage in his eyes. There was no denying that he hated me. My only question was what had I done wrong in his opinion this time.

"This is all her fault," Noah said pointing at me. "It always is and always will be."

"What is her fault?" Kevin responded.

"That Uncle Camp is dead!" he yelled. "All she cares about is money and now my uncle is dead! I hate her!"

I bit down on my bottom lip, trying to prevent myself from crying.

"Son, your mother wasn't responsible for my brother being murdered. She isn't responsible for any of this shit! If anything, she's done all she can to protect this family but shit happens. It's the nature of the business and now we got to stick together and deal with it." He alternated his stare between Noah and Melo. "And you're both old enough to know what I'm talking about. No more sugarcoating. This family deals coke and as a result, someone we loved died."

"Yes she is responsible!" Noah yelled. "Everything she fucking touches rots! She killed Aunt Bunny and she tried to kill you too, dad. Aunt Bunny laid it all out in the letter she wrote me before she died."

I could feel Ramirez and Bradley look at me and I felt uncomfortable.

"Son, I don't know why you think your mother would be responsible for killing Aunt Bunny but it's not true," he lied. "And whoever told you that, including your deceased aunt Bunny, is a fucking liar."

Upon hearing Kevin's response, my heartbeat increased. I had to look over at him because he was saying a lie that he knew to be untrue so calmly that if we hadn't spoke about it, I would've believed him.

Noah wiped the tears from his face and looked at all of us. "One of these days, ya'll are going to realize that Bambi is evil," he said, calling me by my name as if I were not his mother. "When it happens I'm going to laugh in all of your faces." He rushed out of the front door without another word.

I was about to go behind him when Melo said, "I'll go get him, ma."

I walked up to the door before letting him leave. Looking up into his eyes, I put my hands on the sides of his shoulders. "It's dangerous out there now, son. *Very* dangerous." I put one hand on his cheek. "Don't leave the property, Melo. Bring him back but if he refuses to return, let him go alone. I can't have something happening to both of you."

"I love you, ma. Always will." He kissed me on the forehead and walked out.

MELO and NOAH

Melo and Noah were sitting in a small bar in a rural area in Virginia. Both brothers were feeling a little buzzed since they took several shots of Hennessey. Although they were not yet 21, the bar only cared about money, not age.

Things were serene now.

As if they never got into an argument, they talked about everything from college to girls.

Melo knew his brother and he knew how to calm him down before having a tough conversation. Melo tried to adjust the collar on the shirt he was wearing. Since Noah pulled it, it was stretched out and hanging off his right shoulder.

"Here, man," Noah said taking off the white t-shirt he was wearing. "Wear this."

"I'm fine," Melo said with an extended hand.

"Take the shirt, man," Noah persisted. "You look ridiculous."

They laughed.

Melo took his blue shirt off and handed it to Noah who sat it on the bar. He slid on the white one. A few more moments passed between them. "Why do you hate ma so much?" Melo asked. "For real."

Noah looked over at his twin who had the same face and shook his head. "You really know how to fuck up a wet dream." He scratched his chest through his wife beater before grabbing a beer off the bar.

"I just wanna know, man," Melo continued. "Why the hate against your own mother?"

He sighed. "I don't know." He shrugged. "Maybe it's the fact that she hates me back."

Melo's eyebrows rose. "She doesn't hate you."

Noah laughed. "Me and you both know that ma don't fuck with me. I think I remind her more of dad and you remind her of herself. That's why ya'll get along so well."

"So you calling me a female?" Melo chuckled.

"I'm just stating the truth." Noah rubbed his jaw. "And you far from a female, nigga. You landed a good one on me." He paused. "I didn't know you hit so hard."

Melo chuckled before getting serious. "Listen, man, ma is going through a lot. With Uncle Camp being murdered, she's going to need support. You know she was an alcoholic and I don't want her backsliding because she thinks we don't have her back."

Noah sighed. "She'll be fine."

"I'm serious, man," Melo pleaded. "Just be easy on—"

Melo's statement was cut short when a black bag was draped over his head. When he heard his brother yelling, he figured the same thing was happening to him.

Melo couldn't believe it.

They were being kidnapped, in a public bar, in broad daylight.

Although the dark hood remained over Melo's face, he could feel the damp grass against his knees. He was trying to connect to his environment. Doing his best to remember the slightest details in case he made it out of the situation alive.

After about five minutes, there was laughter amongst the kidnappers and Melo felt awkward. How could they be so lackadaisical while their lives hung in the balance? All Melo could do was worry about his brother.

He contemplated screaming but his throat hurt so badly due to the yelling he'd done hours earlier that it would be useless. No audible sound would exit his mouth.

When Melo heard a bottle of champagne pop, anger coursed through his body.

Iakov clanked his glass against Arkadi's before pouring the drink down his throat. Iakov snatched the hood off Melo's head. "Any last words, Kennedy?" he asked him.

"Yes," Melo said as a single tear rolled down his face. "When my parents find out what happened to me you will experience the worst murder you can imagine. I guarantee it."

Iakov laughed although something in his eyes told him that Melo believed every last word he was saying.

"Do it, brother," Iakov said to Arkadi. "Kill them both and get your revenge."

Before Arkadi shot Noah, he said something that rocked Melo's core. He was unable to think about it long because after Noah was finished, Arkadi moved to Melo, putting a bullet in his head.

CHAPTER TWENTY-SIX
DENIM

Smoking paper planes, I was sitting in the living room, waiting for word on our attack on the Russians. We made a few moves out in the streets to strike back but now it was out of our hands. We were waiting on the word from our soldiers out in the field. We were waiting to see if anyone else we cared about got hurt. And we were waiting on Melo and Noah to return home.

"Roman, I'm counting on you to carry things through," Bambi said as she held the phone tightly in her hand. "Let me know if they show up anywhere." She nodded before hanging up and walking over to the table where we were sitting.

"No word yet?" I asked.

"She said she'd let us know if she sees Iakov or Arkadi. But she also said she got word that they, along with Vito, Derrick and Jim, were in hiding."

"Why would they be in hiding?" I asked.

"I don't know," she said lowering her head. "The only reason I could imagine is because they did something that they want to get far away from. Like hurting my children."

Silence.

"I can't believe this is happening," Kevin sighed. "In all of my years in the drug game, I've never been in a situation like this. Too much going on to grieve for my brother. And too angry to do it even if I had time." He looked at all of us. "If the boys don't get back within the hour we'll have to go looking for them."

I gazed over at Bambi and she appeared frozen. I never saw her this quiet. She looked weak and un-threatening. Whether it was Noah saying that every-thing that happened with our family recently was her fault, or not knowing where they were, at the moment my friend was fragile.

I knew my observation was right when Kevin walked over to her and pulled her into his arms. She howled loudly and my heart ripped. When I looked over at Scarlett, she was looking at the table. Tears from her eyes splashed against the surface. I knew her mind was still with Camp and I couldn't blame her.

I was starting to realize that this dope business was not worth the repercussions.

"So ya'll don't know where them boys at yet?" my mother said sliding into the room. "Niggas is drop-ping like flies around here."

It was so quiet you could hear a pin spin.

"I don't know what it is about you Kennedys," she continued. "Can't run an operation and can't save your own people. And tell me something, what is it about ya'll that makes you keep losing kids? First Jasmine, then Master and now the twins," she con-tinued. "Is no one safe around you fake ass gang-sters?"

I finally understood what it meant to see black. Because when I snapped and came to, my mother's meaty throat was in the palms of my hands. She was lying on the floor and I was slapping and stealing her in the face at the same time.

Now that I think about it, the last time I experi-enced something similar I was kicking Grainger's ass. They must have known what to say to get me to go to the next level.

My mother must've been scared because instead of fighting me back, she pulled her arms over her face so that the only things I could hit were the backs of her arms and elbows.

There were lots of reasons for my anger. I beat her for allowing a man's absence to hit her so hard that she no longer cared about her own children. That she ate so much that she gained over 300 pounds and could barely get out of bed most days. I beat her for allowing men to use her body as a playground, leaving dirty condoms and other things inside of her when they were done as if she were a trashcan. I beat her for not showing me what a strong woman looked like and for loving my sister more than me. For making me pay for a gastric bypass surgery only for her to regain all of the weight.

I beat her for her evil comments about my daughter and for not respecting my marriage. But most of all, I beat her because I was afraid that if I stayed around her, I would be just like her.

I was still pummeling her when I was suddenly whisked up. When I turned around, I saw that it was my husband who had me in his clutch and I was surprised.

Kevin and Ramirez helped my bloody mother up and walked away once she was on her feet. She was standing in the middle of the dining room. Her on one side and me and my family on the other. In that moment, it seemed poetic.

She was no longer my family.

They were.

And she had to go.

"All of my life, you've made me hate you," I said softly. "Even when I tried to love you, you reminded me why I shouldn't." Tears poured down my face. "But I'm tired of it, mama. Tired of being the punching bag in your life because you're too afraid to look at your own shit and deal with it. I'm tired of believing in you despite you never believing in me. From here on out, I will not allow you to hurt me anymore. You have to leave."

She looked at me and then at my family. "You already said that, Denim," she said huffing and puffing. "I'm leaving in a few weeks. Remember?"

"No, mama. You leaving right now."

Her jaw dropped. "So you would throw me out on the streets at a time like this? When ya'll got some crazed white boys looking for you?"

I could've answered her question verbally. Instead, I strolled to the front door. Before opening it, I held the cool doorknob in my hand to be sure this was what I wanted to do. When I was certain, I pulled it.

A cool breeze rushed inside. "Leave now."

Her eyes widened and I saw her chest rising and falling. "Denim, if you do this, I'm going to kill myself and it will all be your fault! Do you hear me?"

"Get out, Sarah," Bradley said. "We can't help you anymore. Now go!"

She looked at me and my family and I thought she was about to leave. Instead, she flopped on the floor. "I'm not going anywhere! I'm scared! Please! Don't put me out."

I looked at Bradley and my brothers-in-law. "Pick her up and throw her the fuck out," I demanded. "I'm done with this chick."

I was sitting on a chair in my room. Alone. Dressed in an all black tracksuit, I was thinking about what I just did to my mother. Not even twenty minutes later, I was already doubting my decision. My mind told me that I made the right move but my heart called me a betrayer.

When the bedroom door opened, Bradley walked inside. Instead of approaching me, he stood by the door. "You ready to go search for the twins, baby?"

I nodded although I knew it was a lie.

He came further inside and dropped to his knees. Looking up at me, his eyes light pink from crying over the loss of his brother. With only silence between us, he placed his head on my lap as if he were my child. Reminding me that no matter what, we had each other.

"Did I make the right decision?" I asked. "By throwing her out? I need the truth, outside of what you feel about her."

He looked up at me. "Yes, Denim. You decided right. She was not good for you and she was not good for this family right now. You don't come in someone else's home and throw some bullshit out about people dying. At a time like this! When shit is so sensitive. We don't even know where my nephews are. She was wrong."

"I know, but it hurts."

"Baby, never keep time with bitter people. Because soon you will be as sour as they are."

"But what is she going to do out there on her own?" I paused. "She don't even have any money in her pocket."

He sighed. "I gave her five hundred bucks and had a cab meet her away from the property. I also checked with the realtor who sold us her new house. He says even though closing is not done, she can move in now. She might not have any furniture but it's better than being out on the streets."

I was amazed.

Bradley constantly reminded me that I made the right decision to spend the rest of my life with him. Relieved that my mother would at least be safe, I leaned forward and hugged his head. "Thank you, baby. Thank you so much." I let him go. "What made you do that for my mother? You don't even like her."

He placed his hand on my face. "Denim, I did that shit for you. Not that bitch." He paused. "I knew you wouldn't be right unless you knew she was okay. You made a major move by evicting her and I wanted to support you by taking care of the little stuff so that you wouldn't have to worry. We a team, baby. And I want you to never forget it."

CHAPTER TWENTY-SEVEN
MITCH

*M*itch was lying on the sofa like he did every night, hoping that eventually this war with the Russians would come to an end so that he would be free. His wife, who never missed a moment of sleep, was sprawled out on the bed as usual.

Considering that prior to now they lived on an island and she had every luxury imaginable, Mitch wondered what made her rest so easily in the beautiful dungeon.

With her always asleep, he oddly found the attentions of Sarah comforting. He appreciated their long talks despite their different backgrounds. Him white, fit and healthy. Her black, overweight and drunk.

Still, she had become the only person who made him feel like a human being. She didn't care about the money he had or the reasons he was being kept against his will. She sincerely wanted to get to know him and that made her invaluable to him.

He was just about to drink some wine when his door opened. Hoping it was Sarah, he was disappointed when he saw the Kennedy family, minus Camp, standing before him. Mitch stood up and stuffed his hands into the pockets of his silk black pajama pants. "I'm sorry about your loss."

"So you heard?" Kevin asked with a lowered brow.

"Yes." He looked at Denim. "Your mother told me. She's God sent. She doesn't mind keeping me company and considering my predicament," he looked up at the gold accented ceiling as if he were in a Mexican prison as opposed to paradise, "it means a lot to me."

"My mother won't be coming around anymore," Denim said firmly. "And I wanted to let you know personally."

Mitch removed his hands from his pockets. They hung loosely at his sides. "Please tell me that her dismissal isn't due to anything that I have done."

"It's not because of you," Kevin said louder. "It's just that with the war we're involved in, this was no place for Sarah."

Mitch's jaw tightened and it was apparent that he wasn't happy about the news. "So what brings about this visit?" He looked at the Kennedy family with painted disdain. "You must want something."

"We wanted to tell you that things have escalated," Scarlett advised. "With my husband being murdered and the twins going missing, we predict things will get worse."

"The twins are missing?"

"Yes," Kevin responded.

Mitch sighed. "Well, in that case, I don't doubt that things will get worse," Mitch responded. "And however I can help I'm willing. Just let me know."

"We need your connections, Mitch," Kevin said. "We know you have access to technology we don't."

"Technology?" Mitch repeated.

"Yes. We need someone who can run the Russians' names and find out some more intel. Where they work and where they sleep. Stuff like that."

"But I gave you what I knew. I told you the address of their hideout and the restaurant where they often meet. I don't know anything else."

"We believe that you do," Kevin said.

"You all are giving me too much credit."

"We don't give credit unless it's warranted," Ramirez advised. "Now them mothafuckas killed my brother and they may have my nephews. Will you or will you not help us? Will you or will you not assist us in ending this war?"

Silence.

Mitch didn't answer right away but it was apparent to the Kennedys how he felt about them. He threw his hands up. "Look, I'm very sorry about what happened to Camp. And I'm even more heartbroken now that I hear what's going on with the twins. But I don't have access to anybody in the states who can be of service. If I was home, in Mexico, I could." He sighed. "Perhaps you should let me go so that I can be of more assistance."

Kevin frowned and finally he saw him for the person that he was. A bitter man who was unsympathetic to his family's needs. "Naw, my man. We gonna keep you right here. Just be ready to make them calls when this shit dies down. We're going to need another shipment ASAP."

"Yeah, we know you know how to take care of that shit at least," Denim said.

When they left, Mitch stomped toward the phone. He pulled out a piece of paper from his pocket. It rang twice before it was finally answered. "Sarah, my dear. How are you? I just heard about what they did to you!"

"Not good," she sobbed. "I'm in a cab, Mitch. They threw me out on the streets like trash. They turned my own daughter against me! I hate them all!"

"Well do you have anywhere to go?"

"They bought me some house that won't be ready for a few weeks. Unless I plan on sleeping on the cold hardwood floors, I don't have a plan," she sobbed louder. "I guess I have to stay in a hotel until then."

"Nonsense," Mitch said. "I have somewhere you can go. It's one of my homes in Washington, D.C. From its view you can see the monument in the city."

"For real?" she responded excitedly.

"Yes, my dear," he said. "Anything for my friend."

"I didn't think you could do anything for me," she replied sounding more upbeat. "Since you're stuck there like a prisoner."

"My dear, a man like me can touch anybody from anywhere." He exhaled. "I wonder how long they think I will allow them to keep me here before I wage a war of my own. On their own territory."

Sarah exhaled. "I love my daughter but that's exactly what they need. To be shaken up a little. Is there anything I can do for you? Anything at all?"

"Yes." He sat on the arm of the recliner in his room. "There is a woman, who sometimes works for Bambi. The one you told me was disgruntled at the dinner with the east coast bosses."

"Yes, Yvette."

"That's her. Give her this number and tell her I would like her assistance."

"What will you give her if she agrees to call?"

"Money and power."

"That's a hell of a start."

CHAPTER TWENTY-EIGHT
BAMBI

I had a sick feeling in the pit of my stomach. Something was going on with my sons.

My entire family and me were about to split up in groups to go out in the streets to try and find them. It was agreed that Scarlett would stay in case they came back or called. Besides, she was feeling as bad as I was about Camp's death so she would be no help to us in the streets.

Ready to go find my boys, when I opened the front door Roman was standing there. I was so nervous that I pulled my gun on her and when I looked behind me, my family did the same. She didn't say she was coming over and at this point I felt she could've been against us.

In my book, everybody was an enemy.

With her hands raised in the air, she said, "Don't shoot." Her green eyes looked at my family and then me. "I'm here because I need to check your cars."

"Our cars?" I asked lowering my weapon. "For what?"

"I'll tell you everything you need to know later. Just point me to your vehicles."

Standing in my dining room, I was looking at six small black boxes that Roman pulled from under all of our vehicles. "So you're actually saying that someone put these on our rides without us knowing?"

By T. Styles

"Yes," Roman responded. "They're GPS trackers. This is probably what they used to trail Camp and maybe even the twins."

There was something about the way that Kevin looked at her that made me feel like he knew her. But I was too worried about my boys to think more about it.

"How do you know?" Ramirez asked.

"I know because I used these same devices to locate a few marks I had to handle recently. They are considered the most accurate in the business."

My temples throbbed terribly.

"If they know where we are, why haven't they tried us?" Denim asked.

"I'm not sure," she responded. "But it could be the fifteen hummer trucks with armed men that you have surrounding the property at all times. Perhaps they realize that breaking the fortress may be easier said than done."

"Yeah, they would have to be willing to lose a lot of men to come through here," Kevin said shaking his head before taking a seat. "That's not including the ten men we have circling the house at all times." He sighed.

"But how could they have gotten the devices on our cars?" Ramirez asked. "If they can't break the fort they certainly can't get to the property on foot to put them there."

"Was anyone on your property who should not have been?" Roman asked.

"You mean outside of you?" Denim asked suspiciously.

Roman shook her head as if she was hearing things. "I have clearance to be on your property. Remember? You and me both know that if I didn't I would be dead."

"Still seems odd that you didn't let us know you were coming," Denim said. "Just popping up over here is a little suspect."

"If I wanted you dead you'd all be corpses now."

"Be easy," Race warned putting out her hand. "We're sensitive right now and threats could lead to the wrong actions. Like your head being popped open."

"No disrespect, boss," Roman responded. "It's just that I'm not the enemy and I would appreciate not being treated like one."

Race sighed. "Go 'head with what you were saying."

Roman exhaled. "I need you all to think about who has been here lately. Have you had anyone here who should not have been?"

"I can't think of anyone," Race said scratching her head.

"Yes you can," I said swallowing the lump in my throat.

My family all looked in my direction. "Who?" Kevin asked.

"It wasn't here at the bunker. But when we were at the other property Race allowed Mellvue to come into the house," I said softly. "She could've had someone in her car who placed them on our cars then."

"But I was watching her when she pulled up in that cop car and when she left," Denim said. "She couldn't have done it. We had eyes on her the entire time."

"But you didn't have eyes on her car when she was in our house," I said. "So we don't know who else was inside of it."

Silence.

As they spoke amongst themselves, my mind went elsewhere. The realization was more apparent than I wanted to admit. My sons were tracked by the Russians and were probably dead now. My body trembled. I was the weakest I'd ever been in my life. I didn't feel useful and I didn't feel present.

I zoned out for a second and when I came to, I said, "Can you find out where they are?" I paused. "The Russians?"

Roman walked away from the table and leaned up against the wall. "I'll try. But I don't know a lot of personal information about them. Even Vito and Derrick do a good job of keeping their movements limited."

"That's because they have something to do with the twins going missing," Kevin exhaled. "I know it."

"I don't care what we have to do or what money I have to spend. They have my boys," I said calmly although I was screaming inside. "And I want them brought to Kennedy justice. Alive if possible."

Roman looked at the boxes and walked over to them. Picking them up one by one, she turned them right side up. Her eyebrows rose and it looked as if she had a bright idea. "Give me a few hours. I think I may be on to something."

I was in the bed, the covers pulled over my head. Too weak to move and too weak to contribute to the war against the Russians after learning that we allowed someone to infiltrate our property who possibly murdered Camp and held the twins hostage.

But where was the ransom call?

I was done.

Unable to take care of myself.

Unable to breathe.

It had been three hours since my family left when Kevin came into the room in a hurry. He pulled the sheets off of my face. "Baby, come into the living room. Roman is here."

"Does she have my kids?"

"No. But she does have some information you'll want to hear."

Slowly I pulled myself to the living room. Roman was there talking to the rest of the family. When I came out she walked over to me carefully and stopped. I guess she could tell I was in a fragile state and that made me dangerous.

"Have you found the Russians?" I asked softly.

"No but I discovered where they hold their new meetings," she said confidently.

I felt the breath rush from my body. "How were you able to get the information?"

"When I left earlier today I went back to the company who sold the devices. It's a little spot in Georgetown. For a few bucks, the cashier told me that a white woman bought them not too long ago. She fit the description of Mellvue. Although she gave a fake name, the cashier recorded the information on her driver's license. At first I got excited thinking we would have the place where they rest their heads. So I drove out there and got something just as good. The place where they do their business."

"Can we find out where they live?" I asked.

By T. Styles

"She says she doesn't have any more information and I believe her."

The disappointment washed over me.

"Do we have to put eyes on the building where they hold their meetings?" Ramirez asked.

"I'm already on top of it," Roman said. "I had my partner go over there while I came here."

"Any word from him yet?" Kevin asked standing tall.

"Yes," she smiled. Her eyes widened. "They're holding a meeting now."

The Russians

Iakov was standing outside smoking a cigarette. They were having a meeting inside and he took a break to clear his mind. Leaning against the cool brick wall in the alley, he took a quick pull and exhaled. He allowed the smoke clouds to hover over his head. If things continued as they were, he figured he'd have control over the Kennedy King operation within a few days. And after that, he was certain that Mitch was sure to come his way.

He took his second pull on the cigarette when suddenly a thick rope was dropped down over his head and pulled tightly around his neck. Shocked, he dropped the cigarette and when he looked up he was staring into the face of an angry Kennedy King soldier.

Iakov gripped at the rope, his face reddening as he struggled to catch his breath and remove it from his throat. Just when he felt light headed, as if he were about to die, the rope was loosened slightly. His body slammed on the ground and Kevin walked around the corner.

Standing over top of Iakov as he gasped for air, he said, "Don't worry, Russian. I'm not going to kill you just yet. Although you'll wish I had."

Iakov was sprawled out on the ground behind the truck he was transported in. Dust covered his face and the place where the rope caressed his neck was bloody due to it breaking into his flesh. The noose was connected to the vehicle and Bambi was inside waiting on word from her husband before making a move.

Kevin stood above Iakov and he was unmerciful and serious. "Where are my sons?" he asked calmly.

"I swear to you, I don't know." Iakov coughed to get some air due to being choked repeatedly. "Kevin, I ask for mercy even in war. Think about it. Your wife was in my possession and I didn't do her like this. Why treat me in this way?"

Kevin kicked Iakov in the stomach, forcing blood and guts to spew from his mouth. "Where are my boys, Iakov? Where are my sons?"

"I don't know," he said with lowered eyes.

"So you want to play hard to get." Kevin lifted his head and looked at Bambi. He nodded and she turned the truck on. Kevin looked down at Iakov and said, "Let's see if your answer is the same after she's dragged you a mile or two."

Bambi hit the gas and sped off, dragging Iakov's body against the road, burning the flesh off his back in the process.

CHAPTER TWENTY-NINE
THE KENNEDY KINGS

*T*here were miles of dusty road leading to Iakov and Arkadi Lenin's compound. Twenty Hummers filled with eight soldiers each were approaching the land, all ready for battle.

Once upon the property, they were met with armed men who were hired to protect the Russian land. But they were shocked upon realizing that they were outnumbered. Not one of them was a match for the army that the Kennedy Kings commanded.

Not ready for war, some ran and others stayed to defend the outside of the property.

Within seconds, gunfire blazed from every hummer and before long, every man inside and outside of the home was killed.

Five minutes later, the last Hummer containing Bambi approached the property. The truck parked sideways and Bambi hopped out. Moving quickly toward the door, she removed her weapon and entered her enemy's home.

Denim, Race, Kevin, Bradley and Ramirez followed her, tearing up the house in the process. After going through every room, looking in every cranny and searching around every corner, there was still no sign of her sons anywhere.

Standing outside of the property, defeated and scared that she still hadn't located the twins, she looked out into the land. Warm tears rolled down her eyes. "Where are my children, Kevin?" She paused. "Where are they?" she cried out.

Instead of answering her, he approached her and pulled her into his arms. After a minute, he asked,

"What do you want to do now, baby? Just say the word."

With tears rolling down her face, she said, "Torch this bitch!"

Arkadi was in the back of a speeding shiny black Denali after just receiving the most horrible news of his life. That his brother, Iakov Lenin, was dragged to his death on the back of a truck.

What hurt him the most was not that Iakov had been killed. Anything was possible with war. He was devastated that before his death he told them where they lived. They were Russian and he was certain that if the Kennedys found him, he would take the whereabouts of their home to his grave. He could only guess what other information he divulged to the Kennedys, hoping he would survive.

He reached for his vodka bottle in the small cooler in the car. But instead of it being clear, it was red. He knew immediately it was the blood of his brother. Looking at the bottle, he read a passage on the side.

'We killed your brother and you will be next. This drink is on us.'

When a cell phone rang in the truck, Arkadi's right hand soldier answered the call. "Hello."

From the back seat, Arkadi could read his impression although he hadn't spoken. He knew immediately that whatever news his soldier now possessed would not be good.

"Okay. I'll tell him," the soldier responded before hanging up.

By T. Styles

"What is it?" Arkadi asked readjusting himself in the backseat.

He exhaled. "The Kennedy Kings just bombed Vito and Derrick's houses. Vito was murdered and they still can't find Derrick." He paused. "Boss, where do you want me to take you? It's no longer safe here for you."

"I must get away from here." He looked out of the window. Suddenly everything looked different and he realized he was a foreigner in a country he misjudged. "I need time to regroup and think of plan."

"Do you want me to buy you a ticket somewhere?"

"Yes. I need plane ticket for Russia." He paused. "But before we go, give word to execute the hit on Prophet Mansion." He paused. "They took out my allies and now I will take out theirs."

Darkness acted as a cover as Arkadi's soldiers traveled on foot down a road that led to the Prophet Mansion. Realizing he needed to disable the Kennedy Kings operation like they had his, Arkadi aimed for the most powerful ally, the Prophets.

Slowly fifty men descended upon the walkway leading closer to the acres of land the mansion sat on. Confidently they continued down the way until they reached the gate. One man after the other, with automatic assault rifles in their hands, approached.

To their surprise, the iron gate surrounding the land was open at the entrance. The leader of Arkadi's army, a 45-year-old navy seal, placed a finger over his lips to silence his men. He was listening for the sound that indicated that they were not alone.

Feeling as if the coast was clear, he motioned for all of the men to merge onto the Prophet compound. But the moment the first boot stepped past the gate, bright lights spilled on the land, exposing everything in sight.

"Wait," the leader yelled raising his fist at his men. The fog would not allow them to see a foot in front of them and he wanted them to be cautious. He wanted to spare as many men as possible.

When the ex-navy seal saw red dots all over his soldiers' foreheads he knew what was happening, they were at war. Within seconds, gunfire blasted from the Prophet Mansion killing every Arkadi soldier in sight, except the commander.

With the souls of his dead men in the air, the smell of gunpowder enveloped him and a cloud of smoke made it difficult to see the mansion. Suddenly he heard a calm feminine voice.

"Put down your weapon."

"No," he yelled as he aimed into the thick fog. "I'm not letting you kill me!"

The woman giggled. "Look at your jacket, soldier. If I wanted you dead, you'd be gone now."

When he glanced down he saw his jacket was speckled with red dots as if he were a Christmas tree. Slowly he lowered his weapon and raised his hands. After a few seconds, from behind smoke emerged a beautiful woman with skin the color of pure coffee. Dressed in a chocolate fur coat, she moved closer to him.

He didn't know if he was enamored by her beauty or fearful of her quiet power. Either way, she had his attention.

"I am Nine Prophet and I will let you live," she said calmly.

His knees felt weak by the octave of her voice.

By T. Styles

"On one condition," she continued.

Trembling as if he never served a day in the military in his life, he said, "Anything."

"You tell your boss that what happened here tonight is only a fraction of the power I possess. You let him know that I can touch his family and anyone else he cares about if he ever comes back here." She paused. "I am a dangerous woman and he should heed my warning."

CHAPTER THIRTY
BAMBI

While in the passenger seat of Kevin's truck, I was frozen. I just received news that I never wanted to hear. One of my sons was murdered and the other was in a coma fighting for his life. He had been in the hospital for four days and since he didn't have an ID on him, no one knew who he was. It wasn't until a nurse, the chick that Kevin fucked with recently, saw him that he was identified.

As Kevin continued to steer the truck ahead, with only silence between us, I had one unreasonable request. That if one of my boys were alive it would be Melo instead of Noah. I knew it was wrong and my heart ached due to the thought but it was true.

"Whichever one of them is alive, it's still a blessing, Bambi," Kevin said looking over at me. "You do realize that, don't you?"

How did he know what I was thinking? Did something in the way my body hunched forward give my guilty thoughts away?

"I don't know what you talking about," I lied. "Whoever is in that hospital, I just want him to survive."

He sighed and looked ahead. The glow from the headlights shined against his handsome face and I saw a tear trickle down his cheek. "Bambi, you a good mother. I know you don't feel that way but as your husband, I need you to know that it's true."

I sighed, unable to accept such a bold compliment. "Don't say that," I said turning my head to the right to look out the window. "Look what has become of Camp. Look at what's happened to us. One of our sons has been murdered and the other is lying on his deathbed! If it isn't my fault, then whose the fuck is it?" I yelled beating my chest.

Silence.

Kevin exhaled. "Do you know that after all of these years, I can still see your face on the first day I met you? In my mind it's like it was yesterday."

"Kevin, I don't want to fucking reminisce right now!"

"Bambi...if I don't remember the good times...right here and right now...I don't know what will happen with me," he said, his voice shaking as if he were trying to hold it together. "Because to lose a brother and a son in the same week would bring even the strongest man to his knees."

My chest felt heavy. Throughout this ordeal, I never once thought about the fact that his pain was greater. Because although I loved Camp, I could never understand what it would feel like to lose a brother and a son so close.

I looked over at him and said, "I'm sorry, Kevin. Go ahead."

"I still remember the first day I met you. You were at the airport, just coming back from serving overseas." He smiled although his face was so wet with tears that it appeared to sparkle. "You were wearing your fatigue pants and a t-shirt. And I knew the day I met you that you would be my wife."

Silence.

"But I was selfish, Bambi," he continued.

"Selfish?" I asked in a low voice. "How?"

"Yes. In my plight to have you, I never thought about what it would mean for you. How your life would change. I wanted what I wanted and I knew that nothing would stop me."

"I don't understand."

Pretty Kings 3: Denim's Blues   213

"I should've left you alone, knowing that the life I was involved in was not fit for the woman I loved." He paused and looked over at me. "You said it was your fault all of this happen but you're wrong, Bambi. The fault lies with me and it always will. I'm sorry."

"Kevin, don't say that."

"Bambi, it's true. I'm not playing the martyr and I need you to hear me loud and clear. I know that you're strong but I would never allow you to bear a cross that is rightfully mine to carry. I put you into this life, not the other way around." He touched my thigh. "And I could only hope that you would forgive me for what I have allowed to happen to our children. To our marriage."

My body felt like it was going into convulsions as I cried so hard it hurt. My husband wanted to free me and in the process, he made me love him even more. Kevin pulled over on the side of the road and held me in his arms.

I wept for fifteen minutes.

When we made it to the hospital floor that my son was on, the doctor stopped us before we could see him. My knees were knocking together because I was anxious. I needed to know which one of my children was alive and I needed to know now.

I felt like I was in a nightmare.

But I couldn't wake up.

"As the police told you earlier, they found one of your sons in a wooded area off a major highway," he explained. "He was dead upon arrival with a gunshot wound to the head." He paused. "Your other son suffered the same wound but for some reason, he was able to survive."

"But how is he doing?" Kevin asked as I tried to look over the doctor's shoulder and into the room to see who was alive.

Was it Noah? Or Melo?

I wanted to know but Kevin pulled me closer to him and held me tightly.

"He's in a coma. The bullet penetrated his brain and he lost a lot of blood. We were able to stop the bleeding but we won't know if he'll survive until the swelling goes down. But we're doing all we can."

"Can we go in?" I asked. "I...I have to see him."

"Yes," the doctor said moving out of the way. "He isn't conscious but it's okay."

The moment I walked into the room, I felt light-headed. On the edge of the sink in a plastic bag was the white shirt Noah was wearing. Immediately I knew the truth. God saw fit to take Melo and leave me with the son who hated my guts.

I passed out.

Yesterday after seeing my son, I made a decision that I didn't want to live anymore. I poured so much alcohol into my body that you could smell it from my pores.

Half drunk, I made the mistake of telling Kevin about my suicide attempt and he kept coming in and out of the room, putting his finger under my nose to see if I was still alive.

Unfortunately, I was.

Needing a break, I left our room and decided to take a nap in Denim's since she and Bradley had a soft bed and they were out.

I poured half a bottle of vodka down my throat and was just about to get some sleep when the door opened. Hoping it wasn't Kevin, I was relieved when I saw it was Bradley.

"I'm sorry, Bradley," I said trying to sit up. I was too woozy to make any real moves. "I'll leave."

"No, you fine," he responded quietly as he walked closer to me. "I'm sorry about everything, Bambi." He sat on the edge of the bed. "I just talked to Kevin and he told me what you said."

"About what?" I asked trying to keep my eyes open.

"That you wanted to kill yourself." I saw his throat buckle as he swallowed. "Is it true?"

I didn't know what was odder. The fact that Kevin would tell him about my suicide attempt or the fact that he would feel comfortable enough to ask me. Bradley and I were cool but we didn't have a relationship where he could come to me about something so sensitive.

"I just lost my son. I guess I would say anything."

He sighed and rubbed his hands on his thighs, as if he were trying to do something but couldn't build up the nerve. "I want to trust you, Bambi. I want to trust you so much but I don't know how."

What was he talking about? Whatever it was, I didn't feel like discussing it now. "Bradley, I don't know what you mean but I don't want to talk." I paused. "I want to be alone. Besides, where is Denim? I thought you guys were going out."

"Scarlett said that she was with Race taking care of something."

He looked over at me and his eyes appeared to twirl around in his head.

"Well can you give me an hour and come back to talk to me later?" I asked him.

"I love Denim. I love her a lot and I can't sleep wondering. Wondering if you will tell her about Grainger or—"

"Bradley, I know I'm in your room but all I want—
"

My oxygen flow was cut when Bradley reached down and squeezed my neck. The mattress rattled quietly as he straddled me and tightened his grip. With each squeeze, I could feel my life draining from my body.

I looked up at my brother-in-law again and I could say for sure that I didn't recognize him. The vein down the middle of his forehead pulsated and his face reddened as he struggled to snatch the breath from my body.

Desperate, I scratched at his arms and face but nothing seemed to work. At that moment, I knew one thing for sure. That suddenly I wanted to live. I wanted to be there for Noah. I wanted to be there for my husband and I wanted to stay alive to find Arkadi and kill him myself.

And when I felt some warm shit on my leg I was grossed out. Glancing down, I noticed that this nigga had pissed on me.

Realizing that in this moment he was weaker than I thought, I did the only thing I could imagine.

I raised my right knee and hit him in his balls. It must've worked because he released his hold and I rolled off of the bed. My knees slammed into the floor as I coughed a few times to suck in oxygen. Using the wall to stand up, I struggled to pull air back into my lungs. But no sooner than I was on my feet, Bradley was behind me again.

With my neck in the pit of his forearm, he continued to do what he started. Try to kill me. There was one problem. Now I was stronger and I wasn't the victim anymore. I resorted to my old days in the army.

So with him in tow, I pulled his weight toward the dresser. Once there, I reached for the lamp, snatched it with a hard pull out of the wall and brought it down on the side of his head.

Bradley was now on the floor and I managed to crawl on top of him. I was about to take his life until Denim rushed out of the bathroom. I didn't even know she was in the room.

Didn't she hear us?

It was so big that I guess she couldn't until all the commotion.

Dripping wet, with a towel wrapped around her body, she looked at the horrifying scene. "What the fuck is going on?"

I stood up and leaned on the dresser just as Race pushed the door open and walked inside of the bedroom. "What the fuck is all that noise? Is everybody okay?"

Out of breath, I put my hand on my chest and said, "Lock the door, Race. We gotta get this shit over with."

She must've known what I meant because her expression changed from worry to realization. When the door was closed, she locked it and walked back over to us.

I faced Denim and said, "Bradley just tried to kill me." I exhaled and inhaled, trying to normalize my breath.

Bloodied and bruised, he held his head down.

"Is that true?" Denim asked in shock.

Slowly and almost inaudibly, he said, "Yes."

She looked at his pants and my leg. "Wait, why are you wet?"

"I...I had to go to the bathroom," he responded.

"So you peed on her?"

Silence.

"What is going on, Bradley?" she asked with a hand over her chest. And then she looked at me as if I did something. "Were you two having an affair?" I guess they pissed on each other in the bedroom but that was not my thing.

I was blown away by her question because I would never do something so cold blooded to one of my sisters. I might fuck a nigga if I had to save our lives but it would never be out of lust and it would never be one of my brothers-in-law. "You want to ask me another question?" I asked seriously. "Or would you prefer to continue to disrespect me like I'm some chicken head who doesn't love you?"

Denim looked into my eyes and exhaled. "I'm sorry, Bambi. I just don't know what's going on." She looked at Race and then me. "Can somebody please tell me?"

I looked over at Bradley; he stood up and took a deep breath. Walking toward the edge of the bed, he clasped his hands together and plopped down. Staring at the floor he said, "When I was arrested for raping Grainger, I...I..."

"Finish the story, Bradley," Denim said when he grew quiet.

He looked up at me and Race and then Denim. "I called Bambi and Race to have her killed," he said softly. "And they did it. That's why I was able to get out of jail."

Denim shook her head. "So you're just telling me this now, huh?" She laughed softly. "It took all this time?"

He looked over at her. "What you mean?"

"Bambi and Race told me weeks ago, but I was waiting on you to say something."

"I don't understand."

"You understand exactly what I'm saying. When you didn't tell me about what you did to my sister, that shit hurt because we were always honest about everything. And I had to hear it from my sisters. Your betrayal was another reason why I didn't want to have your baby."

Bradley's jaw hung as he looked at Race and me. I didn't know why he was surprised. I had no intentions on keeping the secret from her only for it to come out in anger years later.

But there was still something I was waiting on him to say. That he actually fucked Grainger before we killed her.

"You aren't mad?" Bradley asked Denim. "About Grainger being killed?"

Denim walked over to the wall and leaned against it. She wrapped the towel tighter around her body and looked up at the ceiling. "I'm beyond mad. I'm devastated, Bradley. But I always knew my sister would do something she couldn't take back. I always knew in my heart that if she didn't get herself together her life would come to an end. And to be honest, a part of me is relieved that I don't have to worry about her anymore." She paused. "But what hurts the most is your dishonesty. So I need to know right now, is that the only thing you have to tell me? Is there any other lie in your heart? In our marriage?"

He looked at Race and me. I wanted her to know that he slept with Grainger but it was not my place to tell her. I would leave that part to him. "Yeah, that's it," he said looking at me. "I'm sorry, Bambi. Please forgive me."

I smiled. "Sure, Bradley. Everything is all good."

It was midnight the next day and Bradley was in the shower. I could see the steam flowing from under the door and hear the water splashing against the wall. I was patiently waiting for this clown, even though he'd been in there for almost thirty minutes.

The moment he opened the bathroom door and crossed the threshold, I knocked him in the head with the butt of my gun. Race, who was there with me, pointed her chopper at his dick and we both cocked our weapons.

"Open your mouth," I said to him softly.

"Bambi, I'm sorry about that shit yesterday. I—"

I knocked him upside his head and repeated, "Open your fucking mouth, nigga." He did and I slid the barrel inside. "You put your hands on me yesterday and I'm here to send you a clear message. If you ever do it again, you will be walking down the street one day and the next you'll be meeting your maker. Do you understand me, Mr. Kennedy?"

He nodded and Race and me backed up and walked out the door. Leaving him alive.

CHAPTER THIRTY-ONE
MITCH

S arah came through and he was excited.
Mitch held the phone to his ear as he spoke to the woman he was sure would be able to give him revenge and his freedom...Yvette. Since their first conversation, he already arranged to supply her with enough cocaine to last at least a month in the project she operated.

Now he wanted her to repay the favor. Her response would single handedly determine their future together.

"I need you to get me out of here," Mitch said as he sat on the edge of the bed. He looked over at his wife who was brushing her hair in the bathroom. He couldn't wait to get her back on the beach where she belonged.

"I don't know if I can do what you're asking," Yvette admitted. "If I thought I could, it wouldn't be a problem but this is big."

Mitch sighed and tried to compose himself. Showing her his angry side would not help the matter in the least. "We're friends, right?"

Silence.

"We're friends but I'm nobody's slave," Yvette answered. "And what you did for me you did because you wanted something. I knew that was the case and I waited patiently for your request. But you're asking me to betray a woman who has helped me get back on my feet."

"Let me be clearer. I'm not asking you to betray your friend," he responded. "Or your low level connect. I'm asking you to assist the man who can change your

By T. Styles

life. A man with the kind of wealth that can make sure you'll never go broke another day in your life." He paused. "I know what kind of woman you are, Yvette. Although our relationship is new, I remember every conversation you shared with me in the days past. I know how it feels to have everything and lose it. But I also know that you realize that Bambi Kennedy does not respect you. And it's just a matter of time before she cuts you off. When that happens do you really want to be out on the streets again?"

Silence.

Yvette thought about having to live in the basement of one of Bambi's homes. To wait for her to give her food. To wait for her to give her money and to wait for her to put her back on in the dope game again. As if she were some losing fighting pitbull.

She didn't want to be in the position where she would have nothing again. "What exactly do you want me to do?"

"Set up a meeting with the Kennedys. Make sure it's actually here, in the bunker. Use a van and have some of your people come with you. It's important that you're in the same van because that's the only way you can get clearance to get onto the property. You'll have to drive yourself and have the men hiding in the back."

"And then?"

"You enter the property and find me."

"By find you, do you mean come in blazing?"

"Yes."

"So you want me to go to war with the Kennedys in their own home?" She paused. "Because that's a suicide attempt."

"They are not going to be expecting you to go to war on their turf. With the loss of Camp and the boy, they are vulnerable. Now is the perfect time to attack! There will be no other!"

Silence.

"Did I lose you, Yvette?" Mitch asked as his wife came out of the bathroom and kissed him on the cheek before lying on the bed to go back to sleep.

"No...I'm still here."

"Can I count on you, Yvette? Can I make you more powerful than any Kennedy who's ever lived?"

Before she could answer, Bambi and Kevin walked into the suite. Kevin looked emotionally beaten and so did Bambi. Bags rested under their eyes and their postures were not as tall as they were in the earlier months.

They walked deeper into the suite and Kevin said, "It's over now, Mitch. We defeated the Russians and you are free to go."

"I'll call you back," he said into the phone with his hand trembling. Mitch stood up and walked toward them. This was the first time he was happy about seeing a Kennedy.

His wife, who was normally asleep, followed. "So you're saying, I'm free?" He was so excited even his eyes smiled.

"Yes," Kevin said. "And I hope what we had to do won't interfere with our future relationship. I respect you, Mitch. And I only wanted your safety throughout all of this. We have that now."

Silence.

"You have no idea what you just did," Mitch said with a grin. Although he hoped they took his comment lightly, he actually meant that they saved themselves more bloodshed by releasing him. "Our relationship is intact, Kevin. And I want to thank you so much for saving me and my wife during these dark days." He paused. "I might not have agreed with your methods but I respect them now."

He shook Bambi and Kevin's hands. "So what's next?"

"We have a car waiting outside for you," Bambi said. "He'll take you to the air strip where you can board one of your jets." She paused. "And to be sure you get there safely, I'm coming with you."

Mitch sat in the backseat with his wife who was asleep on his arm. The sky was brilliant purple indicating that night was approaching. Bambi was in the passenger seat and Race was driving quietly down the road.

Suddenly something hit Mitch. Every bone in his body seemed to tremble even though both Bambi and Race remained silent the entire drive. "You're not taking me to the airport, are you?"

Race looked at Bambi and she looked back at him through the rearview mirror. "No," Race said plainly.

"But...but why?" he asked huffing and puffing. "I've made you a multi-millionaire, Bambi!" he continued, looking at her. "I have taken care of your family when you needed me the most and this is how you repay me?" He paused. "Does Kevin know about this?"

"No, he doesn't."

Hearing the anxiousness in her husband's voice, his wife sat up and rubbed her eyes. "What's going on, Mitch?" she asked.

Race pulled over to the side of the road and drove threw a path that was hidden by trees. She parked the car and looked at Bambi.

"I don't trust you, Mitch," Bambi explained. "And I don't let people get away from me anymore who I don't trust. Especially now. You see, I did that before and now one of my sons is dead. So releasing you would become a problem for me later. And I can't have that. I have one boy alive and I need him to stay that way."

"But what about the operation?" he yelled. "I provide you with the purest cocaine ever. If you kill me, your business will suffer. You need me to run things! Don't make an unprofessional move based on your emotions."

Bambi laughed. "Nigga, I don't love you." She paused. "And since you've been in my possession, you've given Sarge the authority to act in your absence. As far as your people know, he will continue to do so until you give the word."

"So you're going to pretend that I'm still alive? Held up in your house like some slave? No one will believe you forever! Someone will come looking for me and they will be far more dangerous people."

"I'll pull that trigger when it's time," Bambi responded.

"You've been planning this the entire time I've been in your home. Haven't you?"

"Yes," she said matter-of-factly. "Goodbye, Mitch. May your soul fly free in Mexico."

Mitch's wife whimpered as Bambi and Race turned around and fired into the backseat. Killing Mitch and his spouse instantly.

EPILOGUE
THE BUNKER

Bambi and Kevin walked into Melo's bedroom to check on him. After two weeks in a coma, he was finally home from the hospital. He made it. He was alive.

Standing by his bedside, Bambi took a seat and held Melo's hand firmly in hers.

As in the days past, a helicopter circled overhead. Although it was more frequent than usual, they were used to it. A landing strip a few miles away from the gated property brought in many visitors.

Despite the tragic events, the best part about the ordeal was the son she thought was dead, the one who loved her, was actually alive. It was a guilty thought that Bambi kept to herself. She wanted both of her boys but if she had to choose, the decision would be easy.

"Hey, son," Kevin said as he leaned in and gave Melo some dap. His touch was careful because he wasn't trying to hurt him since he just got out of the coma. "How are you?"

"I'm making it, pops," he said softly.

Bambi touched the top of Melo's hand and smiled. "You hungry? Want anything at all?"

Melo rubbed his belly. "Actually yeah," he grinned. "I could go for some of your fried chicken."

Bambi giggled. "You got it, son."

She was about to leave out to prepare his food when Melo said, "Dad, you mind if I talk to ma alone?"

"Of course not, son. I'll be out there if you need me. Just hit the intercom button."

Melo smiled and Kevin strutted out with his hands in his pockets.

Focusing on Bambi, he gripped her hand and said, "I didn't know if I should say this now or later but I think it's the right time." He exhaled.

"What is it, Melo? You're worrying me."

"I wanted to tell you that Noah loved you, ma. He just didn't know how to say it."

Bambi shook her head, unable to deal with the pain of losing Noah and of hearing his words, which she believed to be untrue. "Melo, try not to worry about—"

"It's true, ma," he said interrupting her sentence. "He cared about you a lot. And the last thing he said before he was shot was, 'Mama, I'm sorry. I love you.'"

Bambi's eyes widened. "Melo, please don't try and do this for me. I'm finally trying to make sense of my failures. And this is not necessary..."

He reached up and wiped the tears off her face with his thumb. "Mama, I wouldn't lie to you. He loved you and he wasn't able to express himself."

"But what about all of those things he said to me? On the last night I saw you both?"

Melo smiled. "You still don't remember do you?"

With raised eyebrows she asked, "Remember what?"

"The day before that event it was our birthday," he said. "And even though he didn't say it, I think it hurt him that you and pops forgot. He was a big kid who was looking forward to the cake you always bake for us before Uncle Camp died and it didn't happen."

Bambi felt like she was struck by a dump truck. Their birthday slipped her mind before that moment.

With her hand covering her mouth, she said, "I'm so sorry, Melo."

Her fingers trembled against her lips. How could she be so careless?

"Ma, I don't want you to be sorry. I love my brother and I love you too. I just don't want you to forget about family. Don't forget about why you and dad are doing all of this. Because you never know how long we'll be here." He paused. "Familia first. Always."

Bambi's heart thumped around in her chest. She had a moment of clarity in the worst way imaginable. And it was one she would never forget.

"Thank you, Melo," she said touching the side of his face with her palm. "Thank you."

He winked at her. "No problem."

Denim and Bradley were in the tub together. He was sitting behind her and she was in front of him. Planting soft kisses on her neck, he was trying to warm her up for another round of fucking.

But there was something else on her mind.

"Bradley," she said. "What happened to you in prison?" She grabbed the washcloth and wiped her legs. "Were you...I mean..."

Upon hearing her words, he stopped kissing her and pushed her away from him. Standing up out of the tub, his feet slapped against the heated floor. "What are you trying to say?" He yanked his towel and looked down at her.

"Were you raped?" Denim said as tears rolled down her face. "I mean...ever since you been back, you've been possessive and when I touch you on your back or thighs in the middle of the night you jump." She paused. "Baby, if that did happen, I want you to know that I'm here for you no matter what."

Bradley looked at her as if he wanted to say something and then just that easily, the expression washed away. "If you ever bring this up again, I'm divorcing you, Denim. You'll never see me again." He stormed out of the bathroom and slammed the door behind himself.

Race was in the bedroom with Ramirez talking about their marriage. Although she wanted a divorce, after losing Camp and then Noah, she decided that she would stick around and make it work.

They were lying face up on the bed when Race got up and said, "I got something for you."

Ramirez grinned. "Is it some of that good-good?" he asked referring to her pussy.

"It's better," she responded.

"Well I can't wait to see that shit," he joked.

Walking to her dresser, she pulled out the divorce papers. Spinning around, she raised them up and showed him.

"Bay, what you doing?" His jaw dropped as he saw the documents in her hand. "I thought shit was sweet?"

"It's better," she winked before pulling out a pair of scissors and cutting them up. When she was done, he crawled off the bed and approached her.

"Race, you don't know what this fucking means to me. To want something so badly and then to have it is the best feeling in the world. I will never let you down again."

"I realize this is where I want to be. But I need you to be honest with me always, Ramirez. Is there anything else that I should know about? If so, baby, please tell me now. I don't care what it is, if you let me know right now, I promise to forgive you. That's on everything I love."

Ramirez looked into her eyes and thought about Scarlett. Something told him to be real with her and he figured now was the time.

"I'm serious, Ram," Race continued. "I can see you holding back. As long as you not fucking one of my sisters, I don't care what it is."

Ramirez swallowed, taking the secret with him. He placed her head between the palms of his hands. "I have nothing to tell you, baby. Nothing at all."

Scarlett was in the part of the bunker where Mitch lived before he was murdered. It was her new home because she couldn't live where she and Camp stayed anymore. Although the men thought Arkadi killed Mitch, she knew the truth. In a meeting after the murder, Bambi and Race told her and Denim what happened.

She killed him to maintain control of the industry.

Scarlett sat on the edge of the bed and unwrapped the new clothes she had for Master. Placing them in the drawers, she prepared for his arrival.

In two weeks, although the Walkers didn't know it yet, she was going to get her son. Everything was planned out with her sisters. Bambi, Scarlett, Race and especially Denim agreed to help her in any way possible. With their support, she was praying to be a better mother.

The fellas didn't know he was found but she would explain it to them later.

Not only did missing Master cause her to want to get her son, but also losing Camp meant that Master was the only trace of him she had left.

When the phone rang in the suite, Scarlett pushed the bags out of the way and tried to catch the call before the person hung up. Since she stayed in the suite, she alone was in charge of fielding all of the calls and inquiries about Mitch.

She did a good job of it too.

Her professional voice and quick thinking provided the space needed for Bambi to continue her charade. Although drug bosses thought that the decision-making was coming directly from Mitch, it was Bambi who was running things behind the scenes.

When Scarlett finally made it to the phone the person hung up. Instead, they left a voice message. Since it was recorded on a machine, she hit the button and a male's voice rolled from the speaker.

Although the caller's voice was in Arabic, his tone sent chills down her spine. Something about this caller told her things were different.

"Bambi," she pressed the intercom button and called out into the house. "Bambi, come here! Hurry."

Within seconds, Kevin, Bradley, Ramirez, Race and Denim came inside, each out of breath. It took a minute longer for Bambi to arrive since she was in the kitchen frying chicken.

By T. Styles

Upon seeing Scarlett's frantic face, slowly Bambi stepped ahead of her family and moved toward her. "What's wrong?" she asked.

Scarlett hit the button on the machine and played the recording again. Bambi's eyes widened and she fell on the bed.

"Who is that, baby?" Kevin asked sitting next to her.

"Abd Al-Qadir," she whispered.

Kevin stumbled back into the wall and slid down.

"Well how we going to find out what he said?" Race questioned. "Nobody speaks that shit around here."

Bambi blinked a few times. "I know what he means," she advised. Having served in Saudi Arabia, she was fluent in Arabic although she never had a reason to use the language in the states until now.

"What did he say?" Denim questioned.

"That he is Abd Al-Qadir of Saudi Arabia. And that we have exactly one week to turn over Mitch or we will meet his wrath."

When Kevin heard Abd's name, he was immediately aware of who he was. This was the drama he wanted to avoid.

"Who is he?" Race asked in a heavy tone.

"The most dangerous man alive," Kevin explained.

Yvette, Mercedes and Carissa sat in a black Yukon truck waiting for the person they hoped could save their lives in the event a war took place.

Yvette hadn't heard from Mitch since she last spoke to him on the phone, and when she called the number he gave her, Scarlett would answer in his place. Not wanting her to know that she formed a relationship with Mitch, she would always hang up until she realized it was not smart to call anymore.

"I can't believe you got us into this, Yvette," Mercedes said from the passenger seat. "I mean, I'm just not understanding why you would go against the Kennedys."

"Me either," Carissa said from the back. "You got us into a war we don't want to be a part of. When are you going to start thinking about everybody else instead of yourself?"

Yvette looked to her left, out of the window, and clenched the steering wheel tighter. "I know I made a mistake connecting with Mitch but hindsight is twenty/twenty. He isn't answering my calls now and I think he may be dead. Now we need someone who can watch our backs. Someone smarter than that bitch Roman they have working for them."

"Yeah right," Carissa responded. "Good luck finding that person."

"Vette, keep shit real," Mercedes said. "Whoever this person is you asked to help isn't coming into the picture to protect us. You're going to try and have them kill Bambi aren't you?"

Silence.

"What if I did?" Yvette asked looking into her friends' eyes.

"This shit is so stupid, Yvette," Carissa said. "I understand why you were depressed when we lost Emerald City. Everything we ever knew was there. But we run another profitable business now. Why bite the hand that supplies us?"

Silence.

"Because I think Bambi knows I was disloyal and that I was going to work with Mitch. When she met us

By T. Styles

the other day to supply those bricks she had a smile on her face but I saw behind that shit. She's waiting for the right time to attack. She's slow and sneaky and that makes me uncomfortable." She paused. "And like I said, the person who I've hired is just here for protection. Unless we need something more."

Mercedes sighed. "What's her name?"

"She goes by Yvonna but I think Gabriella is her middle name," Yvette said.

"Why you say that?" Carissa asked.

"One minute she asked me to call her Yvonna and the next it was Gabriella."

"Sounds like the bitch is crazy to me," Mercedes said.

"Since we gotta have her, I hope she really is as sick with the murder game as Roman. I've never seen somebody kill as smoothly as she does."

"I heard Yvonna is better."

When a small unassuming silver car parked beside them, it took a second for the driver to get out and that made them nervous. "What the fuck is that bitch doing?" Carissa asked. "I gotta see her fucking face!"

"Me too!" Mercedes added.

Silence.

After two minutes, which seemed like an eternity, the car door opened. Out walked a beautiful woman with a short spiky haircut and a serious walk. Her tight jeans showed off her toned thighs and an ass that a video vixen would pay for.

"She don't look like no killer to me," Carissa frowned.

"Never underestimate a gangster by the beauty of her face," Mercedes said. "Any feature, good or bad, can be used in war."

All three of them nodded.

"Yvette, where you get this chick from?" Carissa asked.

"She was living here at first but then she moved to the Philippines. Apparently something happened to her family and she's here for revenge, I guess."

"So she needs the capital from us to get at whoever she wants?" Mercedes added.

"I'm not sure but something tells me shit is about to get interesting."

"Tell me something I don't already know," Mercedes said.

Roman was sitting in her house thinking of her life. She just got off the phone with her son Sailor and it ripped her apart that she was only allowed phone calls to connect with her only child.

After Sailor was kidnapped, her husband left her and took their child with him to his mother's house. He learned that the woman who took him was a childhood friend of Roman's who was seeking revenge. When Sailor was returned to them, he decided that he could not have his son around her.

Her heart ached not being able to hold her little boy, or kiss him on the cheek. But she knew it wouldn't be this way always. The plan was to complete the one hundred lives contract for the Kennedys and then get her child back, by any means available to her.

And that included killing her ex-husband if need be.

With the Russians' beef out of the way, for now, she was about to take a nap when there was a knock at her front door. When she looked out of the window she saw it was Owen. Her right hand. He looked frantic and when she opened the door, he busted into the house and paced the floor.

Roman trusted Owen but experience told her she couldn't be sure if or when a man would snap. She had to protect herself at all times if she was going to survive. So she touched the gun that sat in the back of her pants and scanned him over.

She would kill him if need be.

Without flinching, "What's wrong?" she asked.

"It's about Carey," he said referring to his cousin and her best friend who hadn't been seen or heard from in months.

Roman removed her hand from her weapon and approached. "What is it?" Her green eyes widened and her heart was hopeful. "Is she back?"

He shook his head no.

She frowned. "Then what's going on?"

"I got a call today. Someone with some information said that Race and her husband are responsible for her...for her..." He was so choked up he couldn't complete his sentence.

"What did the person say?" she yelled.

"That Race and her husband are responsible for killing her. That her bones should be on the grounds of one of their compounds."

Roman stumbled backwards and threw her face in her hands. She trusted Race and to think that she could be responsible for the loss of her friend devastated her. "Who told you this?"

"She said she was Denim's mother and that her name was Sarah."

The room appeared to spin. "If this is true, I will complete my contract with the Kings. And then I will kill Race Kennedy. With my bare hands."

By T. Styles

CHARACTERS FROM OTHER CARTEL PUBLICATIONS NOVELS

NINE PROPHET – From the book *SILENCE OF THE NINE*

YVETTE, MERCEDES, CARISSA and **LIL C** – From the *PITBULLS IN A SKIRT* series

YVONNA – From the *SHYT LIST* series

KELSI – From the book *A HUSTLER'S SON 2*

RASIM and **SNOW NAMI** – From the book *PRISON THRONE*

The Cartel Publications Order Form
www.thecartelpublications.com
Inmates **ONLY** receive novels for $10.00 per book.

Shyt List 1	_____	$15.00
Shyt List 2	_____	$15.00
Shyt List 3	_____	$15.00
Shyt List 4	_____	$15.00
Shyt List 5	_____	$15.00
Pitbulls In A Skirt	_____	$15.00
Pitbulls In A Skirt 2	_____	$15.00
Pitbulls In A Skirt 3	_____	$15.00
Pitbulls In A Skirt 4	_____	$15.00
Victoria's Secret	_____	$15.00
Poison 1	_____	$15.00
Poison 2	_____	$15.00
Hell Razor Honeys	_____	$15.00
Hell Razor Honeys 2	_____	$15.00
A Hustler's Son 2	_____	$15.00
Black and Ugly As Ever_____		$15.00
Year Of The Crackmom_____		$15.00
Deadheads	_____	$15.00
The Face That Launched A _____		$15.00
Thousand Bullets		
The Unusual Suspects_____		$15.00
Miss Wayne & The Queens of DC_____		$15.00
Paid In Blood	_____	$15.00
Raunchy	_____	$15.00
Raunchy 2	_____	$15.00
Raunchy 3	_____	$15.00
Mad Maxxx	_____	$15.00
Jealous Hearted	_____	$15.00
Quita's Dayscare Center_____		$15.00
Quita's Dayscare Center 2 _____		$15.00
Pretty Kings	_____	$15.00
Pretty Kings 2	_____	$15.00
Pretty Kings 3	_____	$15.00
Silence Of The Nine	_____	$15.00
Prison Throne	_____	$15.00
Drunk & Hot Girls	_____	$15.00
Hersband Material	_____	$15.00
The End: How To Write A _____		$15.00
Bestselling Novel In 30 Days (Non-Fiction Guide)		

By T. Styles

Upscale Kittens	_____	$15.00
Wake & Bake Boys	_____	$15.00
Young & Dumb	_____	$15.00
Young & Dumb 2:	_____	$15.00
Tranny 911	_____	$15.00
Tranny 911: Dixie's Rise	_____	$15.00
First Comes Love, Then Comes Murder	_____	$15.00
Luxury Tax	_____	$15.00
The Lying King	_____	$15.00
Crazy Kind Of Love	_____	$15.00

Please add $4.00 **PER BOOK** for shipping and handling.

<u>The Cartel Publications * P.O. BOX 486 OWINGS MILLS MD 21117</u>

Name: _____

Address: _____

City/State: _____

Contact# & Email: _____

Please allow 5-7 BUSINESS days before shipping. The Cartel is NOT responsible for prison orders rejected.

SILENCE OF THE NINE II
LET THERE BE BLOOD

T. STYLES

NATIONAL BEST SELLING AUTHOR OF *RAUNCHY*

By T. Styles